Marrying Avery

Tammy Godfrey

PHOENIX VOICES PUBLISHING

Copyright © 2023 by Tammy Godfrey

All rights reserved. No part of this publication may be reproduced, stored or transmitted in any form or by any means, electronic, mechanical, photocopying, recording, scanning, or otherwise without written permission from the publisher. It is illegal to copy this book, post it to a website, or distribute it by any other means without permission.

This novel is entirely a work of fiction. The names, characters and incidents portrayed in it are the work of the author's imagination. Any resemblance to actual persons, living or dead, events or localities is entirely coincidental.

Tammy Godfrey asserts the moral right to be identified as the author of this work.

Tammy Godfrey has no responsibility for the persistence or accuracy of URLs for external or third-party Internet Websites referred to in this publication and does not guarantee that any content on such Websites is, or will remain, accurate or appropriate.

Designations used by companies to distinguish their products are often claimed as trademarks. All brand names and product names used in this book and on its cover are trade names, service marks, trademarks and registered trademarks of their respective owners. The publishers and the book are not associated with any product or vendor mentioned in this book. None of the companies referenced within the book have endorsed the book.

Contents

Prologue		1
1.	Chapter One	4
2.	Chapter Two	7
3.	Chapter Three	14
4.	Chapter Four	17
5.	Chapter Five	21
6.	Chapter Six	32
7.	Chapter Seven	38
8.	Chapter Eight	45
9.	Chapter Nine	53
10.	Chapter Ten	60
11.	Chapter Eleven	71
12.	Chapter Twelve	75

13.	Chapter Thirteen	80
14.	Chapter Fourteen	82
15.	Chapter Fifteen	88
16.	Chapter Sixteen	92
17.	Chapter Seventeen	96
18.	Chapter Eighteen	101
19.	Chapter Nineteen	105
20.	Chapter Twenty	109
21.	Chapter Twenty-One	111
22.	Chapter Twenty-Two	114
23.	Chapter Twenty-Three	117
24.	Chapter Twenty-Four	124
25.	Chapter Twenty-Five	129
26.	Chapter Twenty-Six	136
27.	Chapter Twenty-Seven	144
28.	Chapter Twenty-Eight	153
29.	Chapter Twenty-Nine	157
30.	Chapter Thirty	165
31.	Chapter Thirty-One	168
32.	Chapter Thirty-Two	176
33.	Chapter Thirty-Three	180
34.	Chapter Thirty-Four	190

35.	Chapter Thirty-Five	196
36.	Chapter Thirty-Six	201
About the Author		204
Also by Tammy Godfrey		205

Prologue

"We need to talk," Ben said in a text.

"Sure, meet in our normal place?" I texted back.

"See you in ten," Ben texted.

I got my coat and headed out of the office to the Coffee Place where we first met. I started to remind you about that day.

Monday morning, I picked up my usual latte. As I left the store, Ben arrived after having an early meeting. I just said, "Bench," as we passed each other and gestured toward where we'd sat the day before. We gave each other big smiles. What an excellent way to start the morning, I thought.

This man was gorgeous. I'd had several Ben fantasies the previous night, including one resulting in a self-inflicted orgasm of charming proportions. I shivered as I remembered the wave of pleasure. God bless battery-operated toys. I hadn't had to bring them out for months. This guy did things to me.

A couple of minutes later, Noah came by, and he came to me, giving me a big kiss. "Go get your drink," I said, and off he went to the Coffee Place.

I met Noah in Aspen, Colorado, during my Christmas time with Ben. I'll explain more later, but both men are my life.

No guy could do what I was thinking in my head, not until I met these two men. My heart does a little flip-flop every time I see these two men.

I resolved to find Ben and Noah's three hundred bad habits, so I could get grounded again and lose this puppy-love crush I seemed to develop over the last twelve months.

Ben joined me on the same bench with his coffee a few minutes later. This is the first place Ben and I met, and now we meet daily during breaks at work. After a month, Noah started joining us too.

Ben reached over and touched my arm gently, looked straight into my eyes, and said, "Avery, I need to tell you something?"

His statement surprised me on several different levels. For one, it hinted that Ben didn't want to go through with the wedding now. Second, I wondered if I was reading about his looks and comments too much. No, he wasn't leaving.

Noah walked up, sat on my other side, and kissed my cheek.

"What are we talking about?"

Ben suddenly said, "We will talk later." All I could think was that the other shoe was about to drop.

At first, I thought I was in the real-life Fifty Shades Of Grey. I admit I liked books and movies when others didn't, but I didn't want to be in a real-life one. I didn't want to be spanked, but I felt like I had two Mr. Grays in my life, and they liked to share me with other men too. My life changed when Ben asked. "Would you be my 'temporary girlfriend?'" he needed a date for his sister's wedding.

Ben asked me to marry him when we returned, and I was so excited I met a fantastic man. All I could think of was the comment that we have to talk, which is never a good thing.

I think Ben read my confusion as he studied my face. He took my hand in his, and I willingly squeezed back to show I appreciated his honesty and to show my sympathy.

"Did I miss something," Noah asked?

I caught his eye and said, "No." he looked puzzled, so I added,

"We can talk about it later."

Ben stood up and kissed my cheek, and with that, he turned and strode away from me with a happy flair to his walk. I think my mouth was hanging open again. My cheek still burned from his kiss.

"Explain," Noah said. When I didn't say anything. "Tell me what he said."

"He said we have to talk," I said.

"Maybe it's about getting a new house so we can have more room?" Noah said.

"Maybe, you're leaving today," I asked.

"Yes, I'll be back as fast as possible," Noah said. "Now, let's get back to work."

This is the day Ben decided to leave me, I think, and marry Sophie instead and leave my son without his dad. Don't get me wrong, my husband is a great dad to my son and treats him as his own. Let me explain what happened and how all this went down. It started at this time, but maybe it was even before that.

Chapter One

"Tiffany, how was your flight?"

"Same as always," Tiffany said, "I am so glad you're going to marry my brother next month. You are such a 'hot' sister-in-law."

"Ahem," a loud male voice made its presence known at the bedroom doorway.

"BEN," Tiffany screamed as she hopped up from the bed and ran into her brother's arms.

They hugged, and I laid back on the bed and enjoyed seeing them greet each other.

Ben Hopkins and I met eleven months earlier at a nearby Starbucks. The next day he asked if I'd be his 'temporary girlfriend' while he attended Tiffany's wedding. Ben needed to show up with a 'girlfriend' but had no hope of getting one before the weekend except me. One thing led to another, and he proposed to me six days after meeting me, and I accepted. However, I kept the appellation of 'temporary girlfriend' because I liked how it sounded. When I gave that title rather than 'fiancée,' people noticed, and I liked that.

Tiffany and I fixed dinner. "So, what's the schedule while you're here?" I asked Tiffany as I put the salad on the dinner table. "What do you need me to do?"

Tiffany responded, "You've got four weeks to the wedding. There are a million things you haven't thought of, but I have. I have a spreadsheet in my briefcase. Tomorrow we are getting the final fitting of your dress; we're going to check out the chapel again, only this time with the florist. After that, we'll visit the country club where the reception will be and tidy up the arrangements. Tomorrow night we'll hear the band live; we have to choose a cake design; and many other things. Please ask me when I have my list in front of me. Don't plan on doing much except with me for the next four days."

She thought for a minute and said, "Oh, yes. We have to talk about your honeymoon and what you want to have happen there."

"You're flying back on Tuesday?" Ben asked.

"Yes," Tiffany said. "I'm worried about Melissa and how she's getting around. She has the seven-month waddle. Plus, I have a job I'm supposed to be doing something about."

I said, "Well, I am unbelievably glad you took over this as my wedding planner. How'll I ever repay you?"

Tiffany thought for a moment with a sexy grin and said, "Let me wear that little Butterfly you have, and you carry the remote control." We all laughed.

I asked for the details about Melissa's pregnancy and how Mark responded to the two of them. I got a glowing report about the soon-to-be father and more information about the baby girl. Mark was Tiffany's husband, Melissa her wife, and Mark's other wife. That first week when I met Ben, it was

Tiffany's wedding we'd gone to. We'd also gone on the first day or so of their honeymoon with the three of them, sharing ourselves with them as they did with us. After getting into Melissa with me, Ben made love to us both. We were invited on that honeymoon trip to Mexico with them all.

Noah came home around ten that night. We talked most of the night. Ben had to work the next day, and Noah came home from being out of town for three days and slept with Tiffany.

I was doing wedding prep stuff.

Chapter Two

I dragged Tiffany out of bed. She'd crossed one time zone to come to Seattle and complained bitterly about having to get up at seven o'clock on a Saturday or eight in the morning in Denver, where the Case family originated. Tiffany got an extra hour in. I didn't see the problem, but I wasn't sleeping with Noah last night, which was always odd for me not to have both men with me. Ben poured some coffee into his sister's cup, and soon, she rallied.

Despite the temptation, we took separate showers to wash off the long sexual evening we'd spent the night before. Tiffany showered last. When she finished, I ensured she'd found the toy by leaving the infamous Butterfly and its remote control on a pillow beside her suitcase.

Ben and Noah prepared French toast for us for breakfast.

Noah had just finished the first griddle full of our treats when Tiffany came out of the bedroom.

Tiffany oozes sexuality, and that morning was no exception.

However, she had on a silk blouse. The way the fabric folded over her breasts emphasized her bust. Usually a C-cup, she could have passed for Double Ds. I thought Tiffany might have spray painted on the blue jeans; they hugged almost every curve of her shapely legs. It was hard not to notice they made her ass one of the most desirable things in the western world without her looking cheap or slutty. She wore three-inch Ferragamo heels to complete the ensemble.

Noah whistled. I told her, "You're hot. Planning on picking up someone while you're here, I take it?" She laughed and bent over to show us that she wasn't wearing a bra and that when she dipped, her breasts were undoubtedly visible in all their glory.

"Oh, yummy," Noah said. "Can I suck on them later, like after breakfast?"

"Dude, that's my sister," Ben said.

"Behave yourself," Tiffany told him. "No sex with me until we get back from our appointed rounds. We can get you married to this noble virgin. She paused for theatrical effect and added, "Well, not quite a virgin; this one appears to be a pre-owned model."

I flipped her the bird and then kissed the end of my middle finger for her benefit.

Ben planned on working most of the day, a non-unusual occurrence. Over breakfast, Tiffany laid out her spreadsheet, showing us what she'd been orchestrating from her home in Denver. I was shocked at the effort she'd put in; I had no idea weddings took so much time and effort. I effused with my thanks.

As the living room clock chimed nine, Tiffany and I headed out the door to go to the bridal shop. Ben had left me his Porsche so I could exercise his car for him. He'd encouraged me to be an aggressive driver of the vintage vehicle. Thus, we reached the suburban shop twenty miles to the north in a little under twenty minutes.

Taisha attended to us, to me. I'd picked a Ball-gown V-neck train satin lace gown with a full-length skirt and what the shop called a chapel train of thin lace that flowed. The best part is the lace down my back allowing, you to see my skin. Then Ben's family all wore this tiara veil. Tiffany told me at the house, but this was my first time seeing it. This was the dress I had wanted the whole time. We were pleased with the ensemble, and a few nips and tucks were the dress will ultimate fit.

We ate an early lunch at the Tilikum Place Cafe, enjoying our Classic Dutch baby and Cappuccino with a cookie and baked oysters. It was a beautiful spring day. I caught a few looks, but nothing compared to what Tiffany commanded in her tight jeans and heels. I noticed our waiter spent excessive time behind or leaning over Tiffany's shoulder, both aware of the view of her breasts that he enjoyed.

The Special Events Coordinator found us and joined us for coffee as we talked about the reception arrangements. She then showed us around The Ruins, particularly the ballroom where the reception would be held in a month. The place was amazing. Next, Tiffany presented the Coordinator with a reception timeline detailing what should be happening minute by minute. The schedule impressed me, and the Coordinator agreed to the content without reservation.

We stopped by the church where we'd get married, the large chapel on Harvard Ave. The church is called Seattle Emerald Chapel. Tiffany told me we were coming back on Sunday morning to see it full of people and talk to the minister. "This place is so big it scares me to think I'll be getting married there," I said more to myself than anyone else.

"You're marrying my brother; his wedding will be big because it has to be. So be happy you're not having two weddings as I did," Tiffany said.

"Two? Why?" I asked.

"We had obligations, the wedding for our people we work with, and so on. Then, three days later, we married with family and friends," Tiffany began. "We called it practice before the real one."

Next, we swung by Lord & Taylor for bridesmaid gifts. Tiffany, Melissa, and Jennifer were three of my bridesmaids, also my old friend Alex from London, and my sister Amy. Tiffany also gave the groomsmen some gifts to relieve her brother of that chore. While we were there, I got sick. I don't think the lunch agreed with me or breakfast, but I had to find a bathroom fast. Tiffany thought it was all the wedding stuff going on around me. I don't know, it's the second time this week. Maybe, I'm allergic to something I'm eating. I have dropped ten pounds, but no one has noticed yet. I asked Beth about the bridesmaid thing, but she didn't want to be one. I guess Beth has been a bridesmaid over twenty times. As far as groomsmen Ben asked Mark and Brad, his brothers-in-law, his best friend Noah, and Doug. He thought he knew one other he wanted as well. I'm sure they will love the whiskey decanters we got them, complete with pure Kentucky Bourbon.

As we lounged around the living room, I asked no one in particular, "What's tonight? Something about a band."

Tiffany checked her watch. "Right. We have to be at a club called Shasta's in Newton at nine o'clock — that's when they start playing."

"Dress code?" I asked.

"Like this," Tiffany indicated, holding her arms out to mark the outfit she'd worn all day. "No need to change." She looked at Ben and added, "Except lose the Nikes and put on some dress shoes without socks! Noah, please change the suit." "Yes, Sis!" Ben retorted with a smile.

"Yes, ma'am," Noah said and left the room to change.

I went to my room and put on tight pants, a tank top, and high heels. I wasn't looking for anyone and wasn't planning on it. I didn't want to look like I didn't belong to the guys in my life. Shasta's became a great nightclub, and the band rocked. The whole place vibrated to their music. I appreciated that it wasn't so loud you couldn't talk to your dance partners, and we could hear each other most of the time at the table.

Tiffany attracted a following. She had two men that exuded lust for her body, and she seemed most receptive to their advances. Both were good-looking guys, but I didn't think either had an over-eighty IQ. However, she didn't seem to care.

As Ben, Noah, and I cuddled and watched Tiffany press her body against one of the men, I had a flash of brilliance. "Oh, the Butterfly."

I searched through Tiffany's purse and found the unused remote to the Butterfly I hoped she'd put on that morning. The small unit had two controls: on-off and intensity. I turned the power down to about a quarter and flipped the 'on' switch. I knew that she'd experience a warm pleasurable vibration focused on her clitoris from the small device.

Ben, Noah, and I both watched as she jerked her body into her dance partner in response to her felt vibrations. I let the device run for a couple of moments, again knowing that her sexual temperature had risen rapidly from my own experience.

I shut the device off just before the song ended. Another slow number started up, and the second guy came and claimed the right to dance with her. As they nestled into each other, I cranked up the intensity and flipped the switch to 'on' again. Tiffany pushed her pussy into the guy's leg as they danced, trying to either bring herself off or end the torment of being on the brink of orgasm. Again, I shut the device off. Tiffany gave me a ferocious look from the dance floor; I rapidly turned the device on and off to let her know I'd caught her look. She jerked her body into the guy again.

Several fast numbers came on. She ended up dancing with both men, giving them sexy looks and even flashing them by bending forward towards her partners and shaking her breasts.

Both men had large bulges in their pants.

We sat and strategized how to use the Butterfly to torment his sister the most. We both wanted her body hot and horny for Noah, yet we wanted her right on the brink to insure Noah would have so much fun that night.

Noah looked at me seriously this time, "We need to talk when Tiffany is gone."

"Anytime you want to talk, we can," I said.

"Not now, Noah," Ben said. I looked at them both and knew something was up.

"I said after Tiffany leaves," Noah said.

"Something up between you, too?" I asked. "I'll wait until Tiffany leaves, and then we will all talk. So, what do you think of the band?"

"They're great," both my guys said together.

Another slow number came on. Noah cranked up the intensity a little more and flipped the Butterfly to 'on' as she now danced sandwiched between the two men. Her hands rushed over the bulges in their pants whenever she wasn't humping one or the other guy's legs. She was in heat.

Without shutting the unit off, I pulled the control out of Noah's hand, pushed the intensity up to full for fifteen seconds, and then shut the device down. I could hear Tiffany moan all the way from the dance floor.

She grabbed both men and dragged them off towards the hallway with the restrooms.

"I better go and chaperone," I told Ben. He nodded and urged me to catch up with her.

The hallway was empty, and so was the lady's room. I stuck my head out the exit door into the alley behind the Club, looking for Tiffany. Tiffany was on her knees, both men had dropped their pants, and Tiffany held two giant cocks in her hands. She drooled as she started to lap one and then the other, slathering her fluids and the pre-cum from the two cocks around the mushroomed heads.

Tiffany would envelop the head of one cock with her mouth, sliding down the shaft until it disappeared entirely in her mouth. Then, she'd repeat with a staccato neck motion, masturbating the guy with probably the best blowjob of his life. She then repeated the process with the other guy.

I had to admit that even I got hornier watching her performance.

I heard her tell the men, "Tell me when you're going to cum. I want you to cum on my face and on my tits." She plunged back onto one of the cocks. The other guy started to disrobe her, gently pulling her blouse over her head. I moved forward and took the garment from him; he looked surprised.

Nude from the waist up, Tiffany alternated between the two immense cocks, her breasts swaying in the cool night air.

Each guy rubbed and grabbed her tits when they weren't being swallowed.

The tall blond guy said, "I'm going to cum." Tiffany focused on his cock until he threw his head back and thrust it into her mouth. He exclaimed, "Oh shit!" She let some of his cum shoots into her mouth and directed the rest to her breasts, using the head of his cock to smear the sticky white fluid around.

As she finished the first guy, she held onto his shaft but moved her mouth back to the dark-haired guy. She doubled her efforts. Noah came up behind me, and he turned the Butterfly on at this point, leaving the intensity about twothirds of the way up. She moaned into the blowjob.

The guy soon announced that he was 'nearly there.' Tiffany changed her approach slightly and added several deep swallows to her repertoire. He groaned, and I saw a visible fluid pulse down his shaft. He jetted into her mouth, and then, as she'd done before, she aimed his firing cock at her chest. Noah put his arm around me and whispered in my ear. "Tiffany can be careless. She reminds me of my ex-wife at times. I'm glad you're not like that."

I looked up at him, "Are you okay?" I asked.

"Yes, I'm just glad you're in my life," Noah said, kissing my forehead. Since Noah has been living with us, I noticed that he has gotten more protective of me. Where Ben is, let me do my own thing, Noah is constantly checking in. Working in the same building as me helps him keep track—he's just protective. The men are alike in some ways, and in others, they are quite different.

Chapter Three

Tiffany came shortly after. She leaned against the second guy as she came. He accommodated her, his wet cock sliding around her forehead as Tiffany closed her eyes in orgasm. She was still for almost a minute.

I long since shut off the Butterfly. It had done its thing. The men zipped up. I gestured that they should go into the Club and leave me with Tiffany, and they both left. I helped her up.

"Are you having fun?" I scolded.

"Oh, yes. I must clean the cum off my chest, or else I'll stain my blouse."

"Do you want me to bring you some towels or something?" I asked.

"Nah! I'll come in. The ladies' room is right in that hallway," Tiffany walked back in the door, half-nude. A guy coming out of the men's room just about lost his eyeballs, gawking at her cum covered tits as we walked by and into the ladies' room.

Good thing Noah was with us.

"I'll tell Ben to pay the bill, and we will be waiting for you to come back to the table," Noah said and went to find Ben.

Two younger girls in the ladies' room responded similarly to the man in the hall. Tiffany grabbed some paper towels, dampened them, and washed the cum from her breasts. Both girls watched open-mouthed. Tiffany turned to them and said, "Always give blowjobs two at a time. You get more to enjoy that way." She slapped her lips and looked at the sluttiest I had ever seen her. Neither girl's expression changed.

After cleaning up, Tiffany slipped the blouse back on, tucked it in, and we went back and joined Ben. He gave us a questioning look. Noah whispered to him, "Blowjobs extraordinaire!" He gave a lopsided grin and shrugged.

Tiffany announced she was still horny and needed cock in her pussy and pussy to eat. Ben volunteered Noah to help her with the first part of her problem. I volunteered to help with the second part. Ben said not tonight, and we walked out of the Club and to the car.

We had gotten in Noah's car; there were four of us. I sat in the back, and the guys took the front seat. Tiffany got in and climbed in my lap, and I got my seatbelt on, but Tiffany was not moving and started to kiss my neck.

As we started off toward the condo. Tiffany couldn't keep her hands off me, and Ben had a problem. In fact, both men were having trouble with it. When we got back, Tiffany went right on Noah in the front room, and then she pulled him off the couch and took him to the guest room.

"Avery, never do what my sister did tonight," Ben said.

I sat down on the couch and pulled him down next to me. "Ben, I don't have it in me to have sex with two strangers. So, I won't be doing it. I have two men in my life who take up all my time. I don't need two strangers. If I want to have a crazy night, I know two men that will do anything I want."

"Avery, never ever do what Tiffany did unless it's Ben and me," Noah said. "Tiffany is passed out on the bed, by the way. I will need help getting her in her PJs."

"Both of you told me the same thing. Did you two plan this?" I asked.

"If you want to have a night like that, just tell us, and we will make it happen," Noah said.

"I'll have to remember that in case I ever really want to get laid by you two, is to get that butterfly," I jested.

"All you'd have to do is ask," Ben said, looking at Noah.

I walked to Tiffany's room and got her out of her clothes and into her PJs without waking her up, while the guys were in the front room talking. I returned, and sat, deliberately slow, next to Ben.

I leaned in and kissed Ben, pulling the belt on his pants as I did. "I'm asking," I told him. He groaned "Where?" Noah asked.

"Start here," I said, "and finish me on the dining room table. That's just the right height for the both of you to drive your cock into my pussy. Ben, did you know that before Tiffany and I came along?"

Ben groaned as I inhaled his cock. "No, but I had thought about it before you came into my life."

Twenty minutes later, we all stood naked in the shower together. I rubbed my erect nipples against Ben's chest as Noah rubbed his cock and hands against my body; "Thank you, both. You were spectacular twice tonight." I kissed Ben tenderly and turned to kiss Noah the same way.

"Whatever you want," Noah said. We were all cuddled in the big bed for a few more minutes, and I fell asleep between them both.

Chapter Four

Tiffany padded into the kitchen wearing her very short robe as Ben, Noah, and I were having a second cup of coffee and eating my eggs. My stomach started feeling nauseated, and I ran to the bathroom. When I returned, Tiffany put her hand on my head.

"Good morning, you're not hot, sweetie," Tiffany stated. We greeted her, neither of us sure how she wanted to remember last night.

"I think it was something I ate," I said. When I looked at Tiffany, I could tell. She remembered.

Tiffany guessed our thoughts and said, "I vividly remember last night. I thank you for putting me to bed." She walked to Noah and gave him a lingering kiss.

Then she came to me, "I thank you for allowing me to wear that evil Butterfly yesterday. I'm not sure I've ever been so turned on and felt so lusty in my life — and that's saying something."

She kissed me, too, in a loving way.

"Do you remember the two men?" I asked quietly.

"Oh, very much so. If you'd had the intensity on that damned Butterfly any higher while we were dancing, I would have fucked them both in the middle of the dance floor. The blowjobs were a concession but just barely. I almost blew it ... so to speak."

We laughed, and I helped Tiffany prepare her breakfast.

"Will you tell Mark? Melissa?" I asked in an aside after Noah left for work and Ben went to get dressed.

"Oh, I'll tell the two of them when I'm home, and we're having one of our lustier sessions — it won't be long. Moreover, I want to get some butterflies for Melissa and me to use regularly. For some reason, other than vibrators, we haven't accumulated sex toys. You make me rethink that omission in our relationship," she grinned at me.

Ben came out of the room and kissed me as Tiffany got a call from Mark and Melissa and went into her room to talk to them.

"I wish I could stay home and have my way with you," Ben stated,

"Me too but Tiffany and I have a lot of stuff to do," as I wrapped my arms around him. "Remember, we are getting married."

"This is something I will never forget," Ben said, kissing me again.

"You want to tell me what Noah wants to talk to me about?" I asked.

"Let's wait until Tiffany leaves," Ben began.

The rest of Tiffany's short visit flew by and became a blur of activities related to the wedding for the next three days. So yes, we had some very satisfying three-party sex the night Tiffany left.

Tiffany left at nine in the morning. Ben was flying to her home because he had a meeting in Aspen for the family business. Noah and I went to work, knowing Ben would be home late at night.

I had gotten to work and had meetings all day. It's always interesting when I'm at work because Noah is my boss. Since he's been living in Seattle now with us, my bosses, bosses, boss, see him every day, but people still have a problem and get nervous around him. There are women at work that want to sleep with him. I've heard them talking more than once. They all knew he was divorced after his ex-wife Sophie came down and threw a fit.

Sophie walked in during a staff meeting and told everyone that I was the reason Noah wanted the divorce. First time I met Sophie was at Ben and my Christmas getaway. We had friends coming and they showed up with them. When Jennifer called me and told me they were not coming I asked about Sophie.

Jennifer stated that she was a BYHWLYF which means Bitch Your Husband Will Leave You For. Noah and Sophie had been married for many years, but the thing was she wanted to sleep with Ben. Sophie wanted Ben. So, to let Ben have his way and be with her I had him take Noah off his hard limits so I could be with Noah it was only fair I thought. After an extremely hard weekend with Sophie, I put her on my hard limits and Noah was so upset he divorced her. After the fifth month, after the divorce, Noah had moved in with Ben and me. We had become lovers. Sophie almost destroyed my relationship with Ben.

After Sophie did this, Noah had her banned from the building, so she went to Ben's office and tried to get him back.

I was waiting for the shoe to drop, so to speak, but it never happened. Ben came to the office. Noah called me to his office, where we all talked.

Long story short, Ben told me everything that she tried, and Noah told Ben everything. Ben called his lawyer and had Sophie banned from any place where I would be working. Anyway, I felt sick after this morning's meeting and ran out. I ran to the bathroom before I started throwing up.

I had a business trip the next day, and I hope it's not the stomach flu. After this long day and Sophie's troubles, I made the guys promise never to be with Sophie again. It's my very hard limit, and I wouldn't be with them if they had been with her. Noah said that was the most comfortable hard limit he could handle. Ben spoke about the same thing. After all the things she said about me, I can't handle hearing her name or anything about her.

Chapter Five

"Bravo One, Charlie Foxtrot, please state the nature of your emergency and the number of souls on board."

Those were words I'd never heard in my entire life. Yet, five minutes earlier, I had broken off an approach into Bedford in the Cessna Citation to sort things out at a higher altitude over western Seattle.

"Seattle Approach, Bravo One Charlie Foxtrot shows two green and one amber light on the gear indicator. The indicator shows that the right main landing gear is not down or locked. I've tried recycling the gear about a dozen times and some downward G-forces as the gear cycles, but there's no change in indication. I want to do a fly-by of the Fairchild Tower and have them tell me what they see. I'll also arrange for some folks from my ground crew to look." I paused and added, "Oh, yes, I am alone."

"Stand by Bravo One Charlie Foxtrot," Seattle Approach replied.

Monday, I'd flown two others from my ad agency down to New Mexico, where we had a new client — a resort in the western mountains. Unfortunately, my colleagues had to stay with the client for the rest of the week. So, after finishing my part of the business, I headed back to Seattle. This late afternoon flight had been uneventful until I approached Fairchild Field in Seattle — just a few miles from downtown Seattle.

As I waited for Seattle approach to get back to me, I called Executive Jet on their Unicom frequency, where we parked the aircraft. I explained the problem and asked that they call Ben and get him out to the airfield immediately.

I also asked them to patch in on the Unicom frequency, David Lafontaine, or Greg Bellmen from the Wichita Cessna Flight Center. These two men were my flight instructors for my advanced ratings and type ratings in the Cessna Citation. They knew this plane as well as anyone I could think of. They had also participated in the Mile High Club with me a few months earlier.

The radio came alive. "Bravo One Charlie Foxtrot, Seattle Approach. You are cleared for a fly-by of the Fairchild Tower. I'll hand you off to the Tower at the outer marker inbound and pick you back up as you climb back out. After your fly-by, climb to one thousand, turn left to three-six-zero degrees, and climb to three thousand. Enter a hold at the Intersection until you decide on your course of action."

I repeated all that back to Seattle Approach and started to head back to Fairchild. The Unicom radio came alive. "Avery, Baby! Ben here. You okay." His voice had a slight panic in it.

"I'm fine, Ben, but I may have to bang up your plane, depending on the gear. You'll need to decide whether you want me to do a full belly flop or tetter on two wheels for as long as I can?" I noted that my voice sounded remarkably calm.

"Be back to you. Hold on, here's another friend," Ben said. "Hi, Avery, Greg here. Can you hear me all right?"

"Yes, Greg. I hear you fine. Thanks for your help. I'm headed for a fly-by of the Tower, probably five minutes out. Ben, will you be there?"

Ben responded, "I'll be beside the runway with binoculars watching your every move."

Greg said, "Play it straight for now. I'm going into the Flight Center to pull a couple of manuals. Mike's on his way in too."

I acknowledged their help and let things get quiet. I ran through the checklists again for the tenth time.

"Hi, Avery, honey, how are you doing?" Noah said.

"I'm worried about hurting the plane," I said.

"Don't worry about that. I'll buy Ben a new one," Noah said, "I can't get him a new you."

A few minutes later, Seattle's approach came on and handed me off to Fairchild Tower. As I looked at the airport from the outer marker about five miles ahead, I could see a panoply of red blinking lights. Most of the nearby fire departments had provided equipment, and it looked like more were arriving at the field as I flew down the approach path.

I leveled out about fifty feet off the ground in agreement with the Tower. I might have cheated by ten feet. I flew a flawless fly-by, folded up the gear, and executed the assigned missed approach.

"Bravo One Charlie Foxtrot, Fairchild Tower. We see your right main gear is down and cocked at about a sixty-degree angle but not moving into position. The left main and nose gear looks normal. If you have no questions, go on over to Seattle Approach."

I acknowledged their communication and went back to approach. Approach let my head up to Ellis Intersection for my hold.

I went back to Unicom, "Bravo One Charlie Foxtrot with you. I assume you heard Tower. You see anything else."

Ben came on, "It looks like the gear door is binding against the sheet metal under the wing. I thought I saw a ripple in the sheet metal next to the door on that wing."

There was some other chatter as he held the mic open, but I couldn't understand what was said. Ben came back on, "The battalion chief of the Lexington fire department agrees with what I just told you. He's a pilot, too, and was watching from the other side of the runway. He thinks the door has bound up with the wing's sheet metal for some reason and won't open any further."

"I've recycled the gear about a dozen times since I got the 'bad lights' on the panel. Any ideas about what to do now?" I asked over the Unicom.

After a silence, the Unicom came to life again, "Avery, this is Greg again. I think I understand what's happened. First off, it's nothing you did. Second, there's only one possible way I can think of fixing it."

"Go ahead, Greg," I replied. The Unicom radio frequencies are often dispensed with the formality of the ATC radio channels.

"We want you to get a reserved block of airspace and dive the plane with the gear down right up to Mach One — even past it. We hope that in your dive, the gear door will tear off. As soon as you feel the Mach shudder, we want you to back off the speed, slow to regular gear speed, and recycle the gear again. After that, leave it down and locked, then do another fly-by. Finally, we want you to fold things up and do a belly flop if it's still jammed."

"Okay, Greg, I'll go back to Approach and ask for some space," I told him. We both clicked our mics a couple of times to acknowledge.

"Seattle Approach, Bravo One Charlie Foxtrot back with you. We want to climb to twenty thousand, dive to Mach One or so, and try to rip a gear door off in the jet stream. After that, we'd like another fly-by, and then we'll come back around to land. Think you can help us with that?"

"Avery, Bravo One Charlie Foxtrot. Turn left to three-sixzero degrees and climb to flight level two-zero-zero. Remain this frequency; we will coordinate your intrusion into Center airspace. You'll be by yourself above six thousand in the block we're putting you in. We'd like you to execute your dive on a heading of one-eight-zero, so we can vector you back to Fairchild for your next approach."

I acknowledged and turned into my climb. I checked in again at FL 200. The approach had me head north a little further.

As they did, I had a nervous thought.

I went back to Unicom. "Unicom. One-Charlie-Foxtrot here. What if the engine inhales that gear door?" There was a long silence.

Greg came on the radio; "We are unanimous in our belief that the gear door, if it wears off, will stay below the engine nacelle. In any case, be prepared for normal shutdown and fire. You'll probably lose all three gear doors in the dive."

'Oh, great,' I thought. Then said out loud, "then I could try a no-engine, failed gear landing."

Unicom came alive again. Ben said, "Avery, don't worry. Also, when you fly-by, this time, you'll see the runway will be foamed. The fire department insists this is just a precautionary measure. They'll keep adding foam right up until you land — wheels up or down."

I acknowledged it again.

"Bravo One Charlie Foxtrot, Seattle Approach." "Go ahead, Seattle," I replied.

"Turn left to one-eight-zero. Descend your discretion, and level out after your run. Do not go below eight thousand feet."

I started a slow half-procedure turn to my left. I lowered the gear as I did and then allowed the speed to build up. The maximum gear extended rate is 250 knots. I slowly advanced the throttles and my momentum built up above 200 knots. As I leveled off, I hit 250 knots and grew the throttles. I held level flight as the speed built to 300, then 350 knots.

I could feel the shudder from both wings as the gear doors started to flap. Perhaps it was my imagination, but I thought the right wing had more jitter.

I moved from subsonic to transonic at about Mach 0.75. I nosed over into a shallow dive, mindful of the load factors I'd be putting on the aircraft as I tried this maneuver—Mach 0.8 — more shudder. I thought I heard a tearing from the left-wing.

I thought, "The wrong wing! Damn it!"

Mach 0.85. I felt more shutter and strong vibrations from the right-wing. I could see a visible shudder on that wing, but I'd seen more significant fluctuations in lousy weather.

Mach 0.9. Not much change.

Mach 0.95. Shudder to start again. I went back on the Unicom; "Avery. Mach 0.95. I'll go sonic in about sixty seconds." I didn't wait for a reply. I rammed through 15,000 feet, descending now at 5,000 feet per minute.

Mach 1.00, then 1.05 suddenly as I slid past the sonic barrier. I imagined a bump and tear, but things sounded strange at that speed. So, I backed off on the throttles and watched the speed return to subsonic Mach numbers.

I went 10,000 feet, going somewhere near 550 knots and rapidly slowing.

I got the Cessna Citation back to 250 knots level at 8,000 feet. I called in, "Seattle Approach, Bravo One Charlie Foxtrot is ready for another fly-by at Fairchild." They had me descend to 3,000 feet and gave me vectors for runway 11 again. At least the weather had held. The clouds were scattered at 1,000 feet and broken at 3,000 feet; I hadn't noticed an overcast layer at 10,000 feet.

As I descended, I called my crew on the Unicom again. "Avery here. I want you to know I did not recycle the gear after going to sonic. I felt a few unusual bumps, but it was rough. I don't want to fold up the gear if there's something new going on; I've got enough fuel for a few more passes, so let's see what the dive produced."

"Fine, Avery. Good thinking," I heard Mike's voice.

Ben came on, "I'm going back out to the runway to watch you fly by. I love you."

"I love you too, Ben." Now that worried me. My best temporary boyfriend and fiancé told me in a tense and dangerous moment that he loved me. Was he saying 'Goodbye? I'll hide my eyes from the fireball as your plane lands.' Oh shit!

"Avery, Ben is scared, and so am I. We both want you to know we love you. I know you can do this. You can do anything," Noah said. "I'll stay here if you need to talk to me." "Noah, I love you," I said.

"I love you too," Noah said. "Now you have to come back to us."

I made the fly-by just as before, with my altitude somewhere between forty and fifty feet above the runway. I did a smooth climb towards 1,000 feet in my missed approach.

"Bravo One Charlie Foxtrot, Fairchild Tower. You have no gear doors at this point. The right gear is still at about a sixty-degree angle to the wing or thirty-degrees off vertical."

"Tower, I want to recycle the gear and make another fly-by."

"Avery, Bravo One Charlie Foxtrot; left pattern for Runway 11. Clear for the fly-by." I acknowledged the clearance.

On the downwind leg, I recycled the gear. I pleaded the lights would go all green.

They didn't.

"Bravo One Charlie Foxtrot, Fairchild Tower. It looks just like the last time."

"Thanks, Tower. Bravo One Charlie Foxtrot is going back outside the outer and making a normal approach to a full-stop landing with only two wheels fully extended. I plan to bounce very hard on the left main, then go around to a full stop landing. Next time's a keeper."

Tower responded, "Go for it, Avery. Our prayers are with you." Very non-standard ATC communication.

Seattle Approach vectored me in a large oval, so I intercepted the approach course about two miles outside the outer marker. I kept the gear down as I re-processed the flap settings for the approach—one-forty knots over the outer marker.

"Bravo One Charlie Foxtrot is cleared for the bounce."

You'll have a significant red-light reception this time — all equipment will be watching you just in case." I acknowledged and tried to relax my grip. Remain calm.

I carefully aimed at what I wanted as my bounce point in the middle market. I cross-controlled the jet raising the rightwing while I held the plane on the runway heading. I cut the power, and the aircraft took a severe hit on the left main gear. I bounced, and the plane started to roll to the right out of the bounce.

I jammed the rudder to the firewall and turned the ailerons to stop the roll — just barely. I watched the right-wing dip below horizontal, heard a terrible tear of metal, and then knew I had no more control or the sleek jet. I shut down everything instantly. The plane slowed down the foamed runway at over a hundred miles an hour, rotating slightly on the right-wing.

Suddenly I felt the plane spin around as it slowed, my body telling me I was on some wild circus ride trying to make me barf. We left the ground again at some point but came back down immediately. I remembered those crazy twisty rides from the Rye Beach Amusement Park in my youth. This was worse, but I didn't lose my cookies.

Then the world stopped turning. I looked out the windshield, but mostly I saw mud and muck. Then the ground dissolved as a sheet of foam covered the windscreen. The fire and rescue men were on the scene.

I quickly unseated myself and got to the exit. I popped the door and then felt the door open out of my hands. A fireman in full-fire regalia helped me jump from the aircraft from the ground. I noted that it wasn't very far.

We ran from the aircraft, but as I looked back, I realized there probably wouldn't be any fire. The engines had stopped, and I couldn't smell any jet fuel.

The fireman pulled his hood off. "You okay, Miss?"

"Yes, and thank you," I responded. The firefighter guided me toward a fire department ambulance that pulled up immediately.

"Let's have a quick look-see at you, Miss. Let the ambulance attendants check you out." I nodded. I was numb, and the shock of what had just happened for the past hour started to wash through me.

Additional cars and emergency vehicles were pulling up to the aircraft from all directions.

Before my escort could get me to the ambulance, Ben and Noah appeared, running full tilt from two fire trucks.

"OH, BEN!" I cried. "I BROKE YOUR AIRPLANE!"

I fell sobbing into his arms as he caught me. Then, I started to cry uncontrollably in huge, gasping sobs into his chest. Finally, he led me to the ambulance at my fireman escort's insistence.

Ben kept a steady stream of "It's all right. Everything's all right. You're safe now. Nothing can hurt you. You did a magnificent job. We'll fix the plane. Don't worry."

I sat on the back deck of the ambulance as they checked me over. I was fine, except I couldn't stop crying for a while. Noah hugged me and whispered I think we should have you checked out more. "Okay."

Noah ran over and hugged me, and I held on tight to him. I was so glad I could touch both men again. I looked back at the plane as the foam started running off it and sliding to the ground. The plane had left the runway in a spin and veered through a dirt drainage ditch, coming to rest halfway between the runway and the parallel taxiway.

All three landing gear had collapsed after the wing tip had hit. Ben described his view of the landing as he stood atop a fire engine in the run-up area. He said the landing from contact to stop only took about thirty seconds and that he thought the plane had made three complete turns to the right.

I finally stopped crying and became pure gloom. Noah and I just sat in the back of the ambulance and watched as the ground crew started to ponder what to do with the massive jet.

Ben was trying to see the damage and get under the plane to assess repairs. Amazing to me, throughout that late afternoon, I never heard anything from Ben other than supportive and encouraging words. I never even heard him rue the plight of his airplane. I guess he also figured he'd ask me at some point how the meetings I had in New Mexico had gone.

Dusk came, with it, some large spotlight trucks, a huge flatbed trailer, and a mammoth crane. The crew used the crane to tilt the aircraft one way and another and work some slings underneath it. The job was messy and muddy because of all the foam used to guard against fire. Eventually, the crane hoisted Bravo One Charlie Foxtrot back into the air. The truck backed the trailer under the plane. Giant cushions were inflated under the aircraft for its short ride to the repair shop across the field.

Ben, Noah, and I walked behind the truck as it slowly crawled along the taxiways to the shop. The crane followed and helped remove the plane from the trailer onto another set of giant cushions. I examined the bottom of the aircraft. I had seriously scraped every bottom surface on the plane. I might have even bent the right-wing. Mud and muck covered the entire plane as well as the residual from the fire foam.

Ben's Porsche mysteriously appeared. I retrieved my luggage, briefcase, and flight bag from the plane, and we locked up. Ben drove me home, mouthing encouraging words and affirming his love for me. I continued to sniffle.

I know Noah, and I will be going to the doctor tomorrow.

Noah kept watching me, waiting for me to tell Ben, but I wanted to know for sure. I want a doctor to say I am before I tell him.

My landing made the Channel seven news that night. We used the Tivo and replayed the film clip several times to study it. Unfortunately, the right-main gear had never completely folded back into the wing; that was why the plane veered off the runway and into the muck. What to me had been a little hop in the plane as we left the runway turned out to be a spinning turnabout thirty feet in the air, slamming me back down tail first in a vast space of mud before coming to a stop.

I realized how lucky I was to be alive. Ben and Noah wrapped me in their arms in bed that night. I slept fitfully, reliving every second of my flight and trying to find some way I could have saved the plane. I got up at five and threw up many times. Ben said it was stressful.

I called Greg and Mike the following day and thanked them for their help. Ben had talked to them on his cell phone while we'd waited for the plane to get raised and towed to the shop, so they knew I'd gotten through this unharmed. They, too, were full of praise and sympathy.

My colleagues at work marveled at my survival. So many had seen the news and watched my ignominious arrival back in Seattle the evening before. I got a lot of hugs and well wishes from everyone.

Chapter Six

I made it to work and to my morning meeting to tell everyone what happened at yesterday's meeting.

Everyone wanted to know about the plane and what happened. I made it halfway through before I knew I would throw up and ran to the bathroom. This is the fourth day in a role that I've been sick. I have to say it's the flu. I was on the floor now looking at the toilet, thinking it was my new best friend. All I wanted to do was go home, but not being here yesterday, I knew I needed to stay and work.

Beth checked on me after telling me I was sick in the bathroom. Beth is my assistant and a good friend. After I was done being sick and having more than one person come and check on me, Beth came in and told me, "Noah wanted to see you. Do you have the flu, or are you pregnant?"

"I think it's the flu or wedding preparation. I can't be pregnant," I said, sitting on a lounge couch in the restroom.

"Avery, you've been with Ben for almost a year, and if you're not sleeping with him, then there is something wrong with you," Beth said. I laughed because I had had lots of sex since I met Ben and even more since Noah came into my life. I sat back and thought when I had my last period, "Crap, it's been two months."

"Do you want me to go get you a test?" Beth asked.

"Yes, five of them. My card is in my purse."

"Why five."

"I've heard of the test being wrong, so we will do three out of five tests," I said.

Beth smirked, "Okay, I'm going to get you some crackers, chicken noodle soup, and ginger ale too. Just in case."

"Thank you," I said. Instead of going to Noah's office, I went back to my office and laid down on the couch. Five minutes later, Noah knocked on the door, came in, and shut the door. Noah put his hand on my head to see if I was hot, and I wasn't.

Everything I ate this morning came back up.

"Sweetie, is there anything I can do?" Noah asked, concerned about me not feeling well.

"Beth is getting me some stuff, and a test," I said.

"What type of test?" Noah asked, then stopped and got a big smile on his face.

"I'm calling Ben," Noah said.

"No, you're not. I don't know if I am, but Ben wanted to wait a year before we tried to have a baby."

"Trust me, he won't be upset," Noah whispered as he sat on the floor beside me. He reached over and kissed me on the forehead. "How are you feeling now?"

"I feel much better, maybe I don't like eggs anymore, or my baby doesn't like eggs," I said.

"Has this happened before?" Noah asked.

"Last three days," Tiffany thought wedding prep was getting to me.

Ben has been having sex with other women I think," I said.

"I'm sorry, I thought Ben was keeping an eye on you," Noah said. "Wait, are you having a problem with the arrangement?"

"No, and no one needs to keep an eye on me," I said. Then, there was a knock on the door, and Cathy, Noah's assistant, came in.

"Sir, you have a meeting in ten minutes, and some people would like to talk to you before that," Cathy said.

"Cathy, get Daniel and Matt for me now," Noah said.

"Do you want them in your office," Cathy said. "We can find someone to take Avery home. We don't need her getting everyone sick."

Cathy has this crush on Noah, and I mean a big passionate one, and when he became a free man, Cathy tells him she would do anything, and I mean anything, for him in the office or bed. He said no, thank you and that he was in another relationship. He made it clear that she would be gone if she wasn't a good assistant. "No, have them come here," Noah stated.

"Noah, it is better to meet them in your office more professional," I said.

"It's this, or I take you to the hospital now," Noah said.

"I think Avery is right, and she is only an employee. You don't have to worry so much about her," Cathy said.

Crap, she messed up this time, I thought.

"Go get them now," Noah said in a voice I had only heard when he was mad. Cathy turned and walked out of the office.

"Noah, you, okay?" I asked.

"I sat Cathy down and told her we are a couple, but she still doesn't get it," Noah said.

"You told her we were a couple?" shocked by what he just said.

"Yes, it was that or having another late night at work and having her come in with no clothes on," Noah stated.

"Wow, I now want to kick her butt," I said, sitting up, feeling dizzy, and lying down again.

"You do?" Noah had a question in his voice.

"When we were hiding it, I held my tongue; now I want to hurt her," I said, making Noah smile.

"When Beth gets back, I'll have her drive me home," I said.

"You have how many meetings today?"

"Just the one that starts in five minutes, and I'm done for the day," Noah was talking as Matt and Daniel came through my door. "Matt, Daniel, you can manage today's meeting without me, right."

"Yes, we can," they said together.

"Matt, I have one more meeting today, and my notes are on my desk. Can you handle that meeting?" I asked.

"Wow, you really must feel bad," Matt said. "Yes, I can handle the meeting," as he went to my desk to get the file. "Get well, and if you need anything, just call me."

"Thank you, Matt," as he walked out of my office with Daniel following behind.

"Matt has a crush on you," Noah stated.

"No, he doesn't. You are more his taste," I began. "He's like a great girlfriend."

"Okay then, didn't know that, but it does make me feel better," Noah said.

As I sat up to get a drink from water from Beth bought me before she left, Noah got up and sat next to me, and I put my head on his shoulder. "Are you sure Ben won't be mad?" "I'm sure," Noah said.

"What did you want to talk to me about?" I began. "You said I had to wait for Tiffany to leave."

"I have to wait for Ben to come back so we can talk about it," Noah said.

"Why haven't you talked to him about it already," I said.

"Ben asked me not to," Noah said. "I've been thinking of moving your office closer to me. I have that office beside mine and a connecting connected."

"Why do you want me that close?" I asked.

"I thought that I could fire my assistant," Noah began. "You can help me find someone like Beth."

"I can do that without changing offices," I said. "Beth can help with the assistant. If you want the right person, you ask them."

Beth came into my office with three bags of stuff and started talking about what we would do when "I still can't find a way to use the bathroom without the whole office knowing you might be...." She turned and shut the door, not saying a word and seeing Noah sitting beside me.

"Beth, it's okay. He knows," I said.

"See, there is a connected bathroom in that new office. It would be perfect," Noah said.

"Are you talking about the office next to yours, Noah," Beth asked.

"Yes, I want to move her to that office," Noah stated.

"Please say yes, we can move," Beth said. "I'll get out of the open area and only have to deal with Noah's assistant. She's a bitch, but I'll deal. Maybe you can replace her with Kim."

"Why, Kim?" I asked.

"Cathy is sleeping with Mr. Dodson," Beth said.

"Well, that's good to know," Noah said. "For now, let's move all this to my office."

"Yes, Sir," Beth said.

"Beth, you are changing offices, so can you arrange that?" Noah said.

"Yes, Sir," Beth squealed.

She grabbed the bags and took them to Noah's office. "Fine, you win," I said. When Noah tried to help me off the couch, my body had other ideas, and Noah just picked me up and carried me to his office. If they didn't know before something was going on with us, they know now. Noah came through his door, and Beth had a glass of ginger ale for me to drink. Noah put me on the couch in his office, and Beth handed me the drink. Beth was five years older than me. She has been married and has a daughter who has been in the office when things run late, or if I needed help over the weekend, her daughter came with us.

When I got Beth two years ago, she had a guy who hit on her every day, and she walked in on him having sex with a woman all the time, including Allen's wife. No one wanted her when it all came out because Allen couldn't stand her. I found this a good thing because I knew my assistant would be trying to sleep with the boss.

Chapter Seven

"Sir, do you want to do the test in the bathroom or on the table?" Noah's office was huge. It had a table for eight small meetings, a couch, and matching chair, and a coffee table, which didn't count the desk, chair, computer desk, or bookcase. His office was big, like five sizes more extensive than mine. When my old boss left, I took over his procession and stayed in my office instead of moving to a bigger office. I did this because there were no open offices, but when Noah came here full-time, things changed, and people were forced to different places.

"A table is a good place," Noah said. And at the time, Cathy came back and saw that everyone was in Noah's office.

"What is going on?" Cathy said. "Avery should go home before she gets someone else sick. I'm telling my Dad." "Cathy, go home," Noah said.

"What?"

"Go home until I decide if I'm going to fire you, but you will not be my assistant anymore," Noah stated.

"This is all Avery's fault. She has been after me since you came to work here," Cathy said.

"I knew Avery before I came to work here. She is the reason why I stayed here. Avery never said anything about you, but that's not true when it comes to you," Noah said.

"I'm going to tell my dad, and he will have Avery fired," Cathy said.

"Go tell him, and let's see what happens, but you're gone now," Noah said. "Out."

Then Noah went to his phone and hit the button. Peggy didn't even get to say anything when Noah went to work. "That file on Cathy, send it to her father, and if he has a problem with it, tell him he can look for a new job too," He hit the button, and Peggy was gone. "Now, let's get some water in you so we can see if you are pregnant."

I was glad Ben was out of town while this was going down. I didn't think I could manage two Alpha males at once. In everyday life, both men are hell to deal with. When it came to me, they shared without a problem. They wanted me alone and got me, but lately, I wanted one for one thing but not the other. I drank everything in my glass, and Beth filled it up. There was a banging on Noah's door, and it was loud. Noah went out the door and heard Cathy's father yelling. "You got her pregnant and then fired her!"

"I never slept with your daughter and never would," Noah said. I opened the door and looked at Mr. Anderson.

"Noah is not sleeping with your daughter, that's Mr. Dodson. Tell your daughter that I'm filing charges with HR. She never treated me with any respect, and it's gotten worse since Noah came here. Do you know she messed up so many meetings between Noah and me that we have to bypass her every time,"

I began, "I'm higher rank than her, but since you are my boss, I let it go but today is over the top. Plus, Cathy is not sleeping with Noah. I am. He has lived with me for the last three months."

"Wait, you're sleeping with Noah," Mr. Anderson said. "He's sleeping with both of you?"

"NO! He's with me and not sleeping with Cathy," I ranted. "Your daughter is sleeping with Mr. Doug Dodson, a man the same age as you. Many employees in security know this is going on. Your daughter is lying as she always does with everything. If you believe she is pregnant, Let get her tested now."

I watched Noah grab his cell and call, "Peggy, we need legal, video coverage, and I.T. to change passwords," and hung up the cell.

Wow, I knew he was pissed off, but Noah is so pissed off. Mr. Anderson grabbed my arm as I went back into Noah's office. "You're not going anywhere."

"Let go of her, or I will make you," Noah said in a low and scary voice. I was glad security showed up, and Mr. Anderson let go of me, but my arm hurt. I don't even understand why he grabbed me. It wasn't enough for Beth to run to the bathroom and lock the door and the door to his office. She started checking out my arm. I sent him a text telling him. Then sent a text to Ben. "Ben, text or call Noah now. He needs you." "Cathy is good at causing trouble," Beth said.

"We are stuck here until all this is calmed down," I said.

"Let's do the pregnancy test," Beth said.

"Fine," Beth went to Noah's bar he had in the office and grabbed one of the glasses.

"Fill it up halfway," Beth said, and I did what she told me to do. After I was done, I got a text from Noah telling me they were going to meet in room two. I'm showing her father that Cathy was having sex with Doug on his desk on tape. I didn't even know he had it. But he told me he had forgotten something and had IT show a video of the office, so I know what I did, and we came across the video of Cathy and Doug.

I texted back that we would do the tests while we were stuck in the office.

Noah called back, "Tell me what it says."

"Noah, I got five tests, so do you want all the answers each time," I asked.

"Yes," Noah said.

"Fine," I said and hung up the cell. "Men are crazy."

"Yes, they are, but you should be happy that you got one that wants you to be pregnant," Beth said.

So, Beth and I started reading what to do and proceeded with the tests. While we waited to see what they all said, I poured water in one glass, and wine in the other. I watched as a test turned blue, another where two lines showed up. One had a plus sign, and two said pregnant on them. Ben is going to freak out and kill me, I thought I drank the water.

I grabbed my cell and called my doctor, "I need an appointment this week. Why do you ask? Because I just took five pregnancy tests, and the call returned positive. I can't see you tomorrow. I'm flying. What about the day after? Great, see you then."

Next, I sent a text to Noah, "You want to know how or when you're out of the meeting?"

"Now, please," Noah texted back.

"They all say the same thing," I texted back.

"Hi honey, I landed, and Tiffany told me to tell you hi," Ben texted me. "I called and texted Noah, but he didn't text back. What's up."

"Try again, please," I wrote back.

"Having the plane checked out before you take it tomorrow," Ben texted.

"Hi, sweetie. Glad you made it with no trouble at all," I wrote back. "Noah's assistant accused him of having sex with her and firing her because she was telling him she was pregnant. The real reason for his firing her is she is in love with his money and mad because he likes me more. Call him. I've never seen him this mad."

"What did it say?" Noah asked in text.

"Positive," I texted and sent, and it didn't go to Noah; It went to Ben.

"I totally trust you with flying this plane," Ben said.

Crap, I thought so glad he thought that and not something else. "I just sent the answer to Ben," I texted to Noah.

"Well, he knows I want to know!" Noah texted back.

"Ben thinks I think he doesn't trust me with the plane I have to fly tomorrow," I texted Noah.

"Ben texting me saying you're not acting right and asked if you're having a bad day," Noah texted. "Now tell me." "Positive!" I texted, "all of them came up positive." "What is positive?" Ben wrote.

"Well Ben knows," I wrote to Noah.

"I'll tell you when you get home, honey," I texted Ben.

"Well tell me," Noah texted.

"It's positive," I texted back to Noah. Not even five minutes later.

"YOUR POSITIVE!" Noah opened the door and grabbed me.

"Yes, but I want to see the doctor to make sure before I tell Ben," I said. I made the appointment for Thursday."

"I'm coming with you," Noah said and kissed me. "You don't know how happy I am right now."

"What about Cathy's baby?" I smirked.

"Doug and Cathy are trying to explain why they were having sex on my desk while her father was in the room," Noah said.

"Can you fly tomorrow?"

"Yes, I just won't eat until I get there," I said.

"You can't do that," Beth said. "How many times have you been sick?"

"Three times and always after breakfast," I said. "What are you eating at breakfast?" Beth asked.

"She had a vegetable omelet today," Noah said.

"Omelets all the time," I said. "Wait, I was sick a week ago at night when Ben made me scrambled eggs."

"When I was pregnant, I could not eat beef at all," Beth started.

"The smell would set me off, but it started with eating it."

"So, no eggs got it," I said.

"Is there anything you want to eat," Beth asked.

"This is weird, but a grilled cheese sandwich sounds delicious, cheese fries, potato skins, and bacon sounds good, too,"

I began and then stopped. "This is crazy. I can't be pregnant."

"Beth, can you order grilled cheese sandwiches and whatever she said she wanted and make it two orders? We will have lunch in here," Noah began. "Get someone to move Avery's office to the new one. Can you make heads or tails of what meetings I may have left today?"

"Yes, sir," Beth said. "Can I get ahold of Kim to come up here?"

"She is the one you said would be a good fit for Noah," I said.

"Yes, She's Doug's assistant and is so much better than being his assistant, and she will not flirt with you," Beth said.

"Well, let's get her up here and see if she's as good as you say," Noah said.

There was a knock on the door, and Beth answered it. It was Mr. Anderson "We need to talk alone," He whispered.

"Beth, can you please do as I asked?" Noah said.

"Yes, Noah," Beth said and walked out the door.

"Alan, meet me in meeting room two in ten minutes," Noah said and shut the door. Noah came over and hugged me again.

"Looks like I'm cleaning house again."

"Alan is a good person and older," I said. "His daughter is a pain in the neck, but she can do her job. Alan's son should be fired because he's an...Ass. I was trying to say. Being your assistant gives you a thing of power. So, if we make Cathy Doug's assistant, it will take her power and make her unable to be around you. She has to go through your assistant to get to you. You would be pissed off if your daughter came and told you a story like that. You be out for blood.'

"I never thought I would have kids at all," Noah said.

"This way, Alan will owe you two or three, and you get rid of Cathy," I said.

"I should fire them both," Noah said.

"I know, but Alan is good at his job and gives Cathy one last chance," I said. "Call it being a good boss."

"Okay, I'll do it to keep you happy, but I want them all gone," Noah stated.

"Thank you," I said and kissed his nose. Then, he walked out of the room, leaving me alone for the first time today.

The cell rang, and it was Ben. "How are things going?"

"Great now. I was sick earlier but am feeling much better now. When will you be back?" I asked.

"I had one of my employees try the same thing that happened with Noah this week. I had to let her go. It happens more than you know when someone is making a lot of money," Ben stated.

"You need to tell me these things, unless you have something to hide," I said.

"Do you think something happened?" Ben asked.

"No, I said you need to tell me, so I don't have to feel like you're hiding something. If you did sleep with a person, I want to know," I said. "Same goes for Noah. I asked Noah and he said he didn't, and I believe him."

"I'll be back by eight. Are you sure you are feeling better?" Ben asked.

"Yes, Noah is watching me closely, driving me crazy. Are you having dinner here?" I asked.

"I was planning on it," Ben said. "See you when I get back. Love you."

"Have fun, and when I say fun, I mean have fun," I said. "Love you too," and hung up. I dropped to the couch.

Chapter Eight

Beth walked in with a woman who was older than me.

"Avery, this is Kim," Beth stated.

"Nice to meet you. Wait, you were Frank's assistant before he left. How did you get Doug as a boss? That's like three step-downs. I know how good you are."

"Allen thought being Noah's assistant would make him want to stay here. That's why he made Cathy his assistant," Kim said. "With his divorce, Allen thought Cathy would get in his bed, and he has a new son-in-law, and he can run the whole company."

"I'll be right back," walking out of the office but stopping.

"Beth, did you order lunch yet?" "No, I will be in five," Beth said.

"Buy lunch for both of you two and more ginger ale for me, please, and I'm so glad you're my assistant. We will talk about a raise tomorrow," and headed for meeting room two. I walked across the big area with all the desks, and everyone was watching me. I knocked on the door and just walked in. "Noah, there is something you need to know."

Noah turned and smiled when he saw me, "What do I need to know?"

"That I was wrong, and you should do what you want," I said.

"I just found some information that makes your first thoughts right."

Noah grabbed the same arm Allen did, and I backed up on him, "I'm sorry, Avery, let's go outside this office and talk," Noah said as we left the meeting room. "Tell me what you found out."

"That Allen gave you his daughter because he was hoping you would get tired of being here and that you would sleep with her, and have to marry her, then you put him in charge, or even give the company," I said. "Kim was going to be your assistant. It was set up that way, but Doug changed it."

There was a knock, and Peggy walked out of the room. Then Cathy came up to us, and she walked into the room with a smirk on her face.

"Can you get Todd and his file, too," Noah asked Peggy.

"Yes, sir," and Peggy walking out of the office. Noah then got on his cell and asked Beth to get three tests while getting our lunch and adding Peggy to the lunches list. They had my card, heard him say. I told her to tell Kim she has a job, move her things to her new desk and hang up. Now I knew what Noah was talking about, but the rest of the room didn't.

"Noah, I told her to buy lunch for Kim and herself so we can all talk about the new arrangement," I said.

"What new arrangement?" Cathy said.

"That was a good idea, Avery," Noah said.

"You are getting married to someone else and won't be here for long. My parents said that to me," Cathy smugly.

"Yes, I'm getting married but not leaving my job. If anything, I was thinking of starting my own marketing company. Still, I know Noah will have a problem with that, so we came up with a better plan, one that will be putting some of my ideas for the employees to work," I said.

"I can't wait to hear more," Noah said, playing along. Still, I did have ideas for some of the employees, like a daycare for kids until they can go to school and then a teen room for kids that have to come to work with their parents on the weekends. Noah didn't know any of this, but I will ask him nicely later about it.

Peggy returned with legal and brought Todd with them, Allen's son. He sat down by his dad and was smart enough not to say anything at all. "Why is she here?" Cathy asked. "Avery needs to leave."

"Avery, sit down, please," Noah said. "Cathy, you been nothing but disrespectful to Avery, and I want you fired."

"You can't do that. My dad is your boss," Cathy said. "My dad is planning on firing Avery as soon as this meeting is over.

"Allen, who's the boss?" Noah asked.

"You are, unless you're not here, then I am," Allen said.

There was a knock and Doug came in. "Sit, Doug." Doug sat two seats away from Todd.

Another knock, and Kim came in "What should I do with Cathy's stuff?" looking at Noah and me.

"Why are you moving my stuff?" Cathy asked.

"I'll go help you," I said and got up.

"Avery, it's okay. Just tell me what you want to do?" Kim asked.

"Put it in a box until we find out how the meeting will end," I said.

"Thank you," and Kim walked out of the office.

"What is going on?" Doug said. "Are you taking my assistant?"

Before Noah could answer the question, Beth walked in with the brown bag. "Here you go. Your office is being moved too.

Do you want to do your desk, or can I do it?" "You don't mind?" I asked.

"No," Beth said.

"Okay, the faster we get in the office, the better Noah will feel," I said. "Can you bring a glass, please?" "Be right back," Beth said.

"What are we doing here?" Todd asked. Well, that was a dumb thing to do as he looked at his dad.

"Well, since you asked," Noah began. "Let's start. I want to make sure I have the facts straight first. Doug, how long have you been in a relationship with Cathy? Before you lie, we watched you having sex on my desk."

"Six months," Doug admitted just loud enough for everyone to hear. "We only had sex on your desk once. Cathy thought it would be fun."

"Thank you for the honesty," Noah said.

"Cathy told me she is pregnant and that I'm the father," Noah began. And Doug looked over at Cathy.

"You slept with Noah, and now we don't know who the father is?" Doug started.

"No, Noah never had sex with Cathy," I said.

"Since everyone believes Cathy, we are going to have some honesty from her," Noah started again. "Cathy has put Doug, her father, and her brother's job on the line. Are you pregnant, Cathy?"

"Yes, and you're the father," Cathy said, looking at me with a satisfying look on her face, but I don't think she understands what was going on.

"Fine, prove it now," and Noah started taking out the pregnancy tests. Beth brought in the cup and then told her to make sure everyone is out of the bathroom so she can go to the bathroom and fill the cup. Beth left the room to get the bathroom cleared out.

"If she is pregnant, then all your jobs are safe with some changes," Noah said. "But if she not, then you're all fired."

"So, Cathy let's get started," Peggy said. "I'll walk you to the bathroom and then back with the sample and see. Can start the test."

"Tests can be wrong," Cathy stated.

"Well, that's why we brought three," Noah said. "Cathy, you told everyone I was having sex with you and got you pregnant. I'm in a relationship with someone, and I had to explain to her that this was not true, but you keep saying it is, plus you have been sleeping with Doug for six months. So, let's see if you're not lying about it."

"Wait, I don't like this at all," Allen said.

"Fine, you're all fired now," Noah said.

"Daddy don't believe him. You say at home that if you didn't work here, nothing would get done," Cathy stated.

"Right now, you have a fifty/fifty chance of keeping your job, but if Cathy doesn't test, you're fired," Peggy said again.

"Can we talk to my daughter first," Allen asked.

"No, you have caused enough trouble today," Peggy said.

"Why am I even in this?" Doug said. "Yes, I had sex on Noah's desk, but Cathy said it was okay and no one would find out, and second I didn't even know about the pregnancy stuff." "You're going to have to get a new desk," I told Noah.

"I know," Noah said. "I ordered one after I saw the video the first time. Will be in tomorrow." "Thank God," I said.

"What are you going to do, Allen? Is she testing now or not?" Noah said. "Doug, you can keep your job, but I'm taking your assistant."

"I'm getting a new one then?" Doug said.

"Yes," Noah said.

"I don't think she is pregnant; I use a condom every time, and she told me she was on the pill," Doug said.

"Shut up, Doug," Cathy said.

"Well?" Peggy asked.

"I want to call my lawyer!" Allen stated.

"You can, but it won't change anything," Peggy said.

I saw Noah look at his cell and then look up at me. "I have to take this call. Let him call his lawyer and call our lawyers in too."

"Doug, do you want to know if she pregnant or not?" Peggy asked.

"Yes, I would," Doug said. "I have a meeting downtown in twenty minutes."

"Go to the meeting, and I'll inform you if she takes the test," I said.

"You have no control here to say he can leave," Allen said.

"Right now, Avery is in charge because you're going to be fired, and Avery will replace you," Peggy stated and looked happy saying it, which I found interesting. I watched Noah go to his office and shut the door. I didn't know that I was replacing Allen.

"My lawyers are on their way," Allen said.

"Well, then everyone take a lunch. Be back in an hour, but Cathy has to stay here until we get the sample for the test," I said.

"This is so stupid," Allen said. "When this is cleared up, I'm firing you, Avery."

"Well, I see where Cathy gets it from," I said. "Peggy, can you have security watch her until after lunch?" "Yes, Avery, anything else?" Peggy asked.

"I'm not staying in this room," Cathy said.

"Then you're all fired, take your pick?" Peggy said.

"This is Noah's baby, and he's lying to you. He had me so many times on that desk of his I bet there is the video of it," Cathy said.

"So, if you did have sex with him, was it this month, last month, or both," I asked.

"It was three days ago, and we had sex many times around the building too," Cathy said.

"Peggy, get the IT guys going through the video for the last two month. As she says, it will be on the videos and have them look at all the videos for the whole building to see if they can find anything," I said. "Have security walk the men to the front door to go to lunch and then have them escorted back to this room. I don't want him going to any office."

"This is bull," Allen said as Noah came back into the office.

"Noah, I'm not going to do anything Avery says." "Then you're fired," Noah said.

"Noah, Avery has us taking one hour lunch..." Peggy began, but Noah held up his hand to stop her.

"Whatever Avery said, just do it," and pulled out my chair, opened the door, and had me follow him into his office and shut the door behind us. As I walked by, I saw Kim setting up her desk, and Beth had movers moving my stuff in the new desk. I turned, and Noah was on his knees. I didn't know what was going on.

"By the way, thanks for that promotion," I said, looking down at him. "Allen said his lawyer would be here in an hour, and I told everyone to break for lunch, but Cathy had to stay with us until she gives a sample or stays in the room until we solve all this. Cathy told me she had sex with you for the last two months on your office desk. I think she was trying to piss me off, but I told Peggy to have IT staff go through the video in the whole office to see where you had sex with Cathy."

"I didn't have sex with her," Noah said. "I haven't had sex with anyone but who you know about."

"Noah, I know that," I said. Noah took a deep breath. "It's okay, you're not mine. You can have sex with whoever you want."

"You're not jealous at all," Noah asked in a whisper.

"I wouldn't say that," bending down to his level. "Noah, the idea of you being with anyone drives me crazy even more so for you than Ben, and I don't understand why? All I do know is that I want all three of us together, and I want to have Ben's and your kids. If I could marry you both, I would because I love you," I said. Noah pulled me into a passionate kiss.

"I love you always," Noah said. "That's what Ben and I wanted to talk to you about. We want the same thing. I promise I never slept with her."

"I don't know if Ben and I can work without you too," I whispered, saying something I thought about a lot. "Ben is gone all the time, and I understand that and accept it, but something has been off this last month, like he's been sleeping with someone else. Something is bugging him, and he's not talking about it. Sex has been different, like more intense, wanting me to himself and locking the door. I never saw him lock the door before. Like he was afraid I'd leave."

"We will talk about this at home, but Ben called telling me you're not happy with us and Ben and I are cheating. Well, not cheating, but you know what I mean," Noah said.

"I know what you mean, and I know you are not, but I think Ben did," I said. "Plus, if you want sex, you just tell me, and we have it."

"You mean we can have sex on my desk," Noah said.

"Not that desk but the new one, yes, and mine," I said and then thought a moment said, "The meeting offices would be fun too."

"I love you," Noah said and pulled me in for a kiss.

"Why did you get on your knees," I asked.

"I know you see us as two Alpha males, but I see you as the Alpha of both of us," Noah said. I had him stand up and kiss me again.

"Well, if I'm with a child, you're going to make a great dad," I said. Then there was a knock on the door.

Chapter Nine

When the door was shut, I saw Beth and Kim putting the food out, and Beth handled me the Ginger Ale and had a long drink. "I'm so hungry," I said out loud.

I sat at the table with all four of us, and we started eating. "Where's Peggy?" Noah asked, then looked at the two other ladies in the office. "You have signed NDA's, right, and nothing we say you can repeat, right."

"You're a couple, and Avery may be pregnant," Kim said.

"I know you love him," Beth said. "I know you're in a polyamory relationship."

"I won't repeat anything. You got me away from Doug and Allen. I owe you like ten dinners and hundreds of hours for getting me away from him and Cathy," Kim said.

"Now that's done, let's eat," Beth said. "I have signed an NDA too, and I've kept your secret for the last ten months."

I looked over at Beth and Kim. "We have something to tell you."

"Well, you shared yourself. I think we can share our situation with you," Beth said.

"You're with Jeremy," I said.

"Yes, and Mark and Peggy, we all live in the same house," Beth said, waiting for the shoe to drop, but it didn't.

"Beth, I don't think they care," Kim smirked. "They understand and won't judge."

"I have a question, but we will talk later, but can I ask two questions. One is how long have you been in this relationship, and has it worked out, I mean with kids and all?" I asked.

"For me ten years, Beth moved in four years ago, and we had some people come and go, but we haven't brought anyone else into the house since Beth and her daughter. My ex will not let my kids come to the house, and since they said they wanted to live with their dad, I do as they want. Mark's two kids live in the house, and Jeremy's son lives there too. Jeremy wants another child, so Jeremy and Peggy are trying right now," Kim said. "We all look out for each other, and the kids are always taken care of most of the time. The girls share a room, and the boys share, but the oldest has his room."

"My daughter calls everyone aunt and uncle," Beth said.

"Well, except Jeremy, she calls him dad."

"I knew Noah was in the lifestyle because of his ex-wife, but I didn't know he was seeing anyone until Cathy told everyone she was with him," Kim said.

There was a knock on the door, and it was Peggy, "Sir, the staff took it upon themselves to start looking through all the videos. They knew you would be asking for them, or Avery would. They found four different people having sex in different areas, with Cathy with another guy. They don't know him but they are looking for who it is. We caught Todd opening mail in the mailroom and then reporting to his dad." "Wait, you have proof of this," Noah asked.

"Have a seat and eat, Peggy," Noah said. Kim handed over the box that had her lunch, and she opened it.

"There's more, do you want to know now?" Peggy asked. I didn't like the look in the woman's eyes. I knew it wasn't right when she looked at Kim and Beth.

"Go on," Noah said as he was taking a few potato skins.

"Cathy has been reporting to your ex-wife too," Peggy said. Noah hit his desk hard and had us all jumping at once.

"Does the video show what they are saying?" Noah asked. "Just put everything in boxes with Allen and his kids, and we will meet their lawyer before we get back so we can see if they want to fight. I want all their areas and Allen's office cleaned out. Anything about this company stays, but everything else goes. Move all the meetings and reports to my office and Avery and me will go through them. Have his assistant come too. What is she like?"

"Allen's bed buddy," Peggy said, and Kim choked on her drink.

"Well, that was blunt," I said.

"Peggy knows I like blunt," Noah said.

"We will make her Doug's new assistant," Noah said. Then Beth and I both choked on our food.

We sat and ate while people knocked on the door and asked what was happening next. I looked up "Kim, is there anything about Doug we need to know?"

"He's good at coming up with ideas but not good at following through.

"Why isn't he on the think tank area?" Noah asked.

"He works with them now. Eight months ago, Allen moved him to this office, and I was moved to assistant. He doesn't meet with clients but has helped with ideas for five other men who are not good at ideas but good at taking the job and running with it," Kim said.

"Explain what a day is like," Noah asked as we all ate.

"The group of five meet with Allen and tell them what they're working on. So, meeting the clients and so on. Then they go to Doug, and he gives them ten ideas off the top of his head, and I must write them out and send them to Allen. Then Allen picks the ones he likes and sends them forward to the group of five, and they take it to the client, and if they like it, then it goes into production," Kim explained.

"Wait," I began. "The top five should not use the think tank or Doug. Allen told me they are that good and don't need the help. Plus, they are the ones always getting all the bonuses. I brought in tons of clients, and these five assholes are not doing it themselves. I brought in the most money and clients last year and was told I wasn't good enough yet. The bonuses went to the men who look like supermodels, but I think they are dumb as rocks when it comes to ideas now, and I know why. Allen kept telling me I was lucky to be in the spot I was in because he would never have promoted me if I wasn't the next in line. Noah knew of my shortfalls but wanted to give me a chance."

"I was promoted right before you came, but Allen likes men in power, not women," Kim said. "Allen has a file on you, just waiting for you to mess up. That's why Cathy's been doing all the miss calls."

"Before I came, I told Allen to promote you," I told her. "I didn't know it was you. Allen was trying to talk me out of it, saying you were too much of a girl to deal with the big boys. I told him that you were the next to be promoted. If it doesn't work out, we could demote you or teach you. Still, I said to him that the company was too top-heavy with men, and we needed to add some women in top places because I know there is a woman that can do the same thing.

"I've always had the best person for the job," Noah said, "It still evened out, but not with this company. I was going through all the sections and changing things. I thought it was an area thing with all the men in critical areas. I did HR first because if you don't have a good HR team, your fucked. I found the problem there with my first day in the building, and the dumb ass acted like I was no one. As I talked to all the HR people, I found Peggy knew her shit and wouldn't put up with crap, but I found the three men in critical areas were assess and fired them all on the first day I was here."

"You scared the hell out of everyone. Allen came to me and told me this was only short-term because you would be leaving soon. I knew that wasn't true when you put in your address change, and it was the same as Avery's. I knew you were staying for a while," Peggy said.

"So, you're telling me you knew what I was doing but didn't help me do it?" Noah said.

"I have a file on all the dumbasses that I have told Allen about, and he tells me to mind my own business, so if you want the files tell me, and I'll have them on your desk today," Peggy said. "Plus, I have enough on the three in the meeting room. You can fire them today."

"Bring it to me," Noah said. Peggy left the office to get the files, and I just looked at him.

"Looks like we will be having a long night," I said. "Ben will be home around eight, so work at home tonight and order in?"
"Yes, Ben is going to kill me," Noah said.

"When I came here, I moved Anderson to Kanas. He was happy because his spouse wanted to be closer to his family. I thought that he had made the changes, so I put him in a company with a great staff to inform me of any changes or not. They love him, and he loves his team. So, I knew it had to be someone in the company doing it.

Beth got a call and left the office, leaving Kim, Noah, and me. "Kim, you know Avery and I are in a relationship," Noah said. "You can say she's, my spouse, and always send her calls through, and for Ben, if she wants me for anything. They are my family. If my mom calls, let me know first, or my father but Ben and Avery are my heart. Ben has sisters who are family, so you can put them on hold, but tell me fast. I'll give you, their names. My ex-wife Sophia is on the do-not-allow-the-call-togo-through-no-matter-what-list. Tell me she called but lose it. Get a message. I have to be in a mood to talk to her, and right now, I am in no mood to talk to her. Cathy always let her

though, despite my telling her repeatedly."

"You know your ex was in the building yesterday," Kim said. "She was in Doug's office with Allen and Cathy."

Peggy came back in with a stack of files, and it was big. "How many people are there," I asked.

"Could you please have the IT tech put a group of all the stuff with my ex-wife in it, and send it to me?" Noah said to Peggy. "How many people will I be looking into." "Eight," Peggy stated.

"I thought I told everyone that my ex-wife was not allowed in the building," Noah stated.

"You did, but Allen said you changed your mind," Peggy stated. "I have been watching where she has been going and have a file on that too. Because I knew you asked for it some time."

"You're in the wrong job, Peggy. You should be the head of security," I said.

"I gave Allen all this information, and he told me to not worry about it, and it's not my job," Peggy said.

"I also want a list of everyone who had a meeting with my ex-wife," Noah stated.

Beth walked back in. "The plane is set for tomorrow." "Thank you," I said.

"You're flying tomorrow?" Noah asked with concern.

"Yes, it was Ben, and your idea, remember. Get back on the horse thing. I'm taking four of us to a meeting in Denver, staying down there for a week. If they accept the deal, I'm flying back, if it doesn't work, I bring everyone back. You said it was dumb for me to stay there overnight because I couldn't get a flight back, and I should fly and be back at the early dusk."

"Can we talk about this tonight," Noah said.

"Sure, but it won't change anything."

"Beth, see if they can change the meeting to two days from now?" Noah asked. "Tell them we are going through some personnel changes."

"Why are you doing that?" I asked.

"Think about who was going," Noah said. "We have to have the people to replace them on board."

"You're right I didn't think of that," I said.

Chapter Ten

We made it back into the meeting room, and now Allen is saying I was pushing him out of his job.

It doesn't matter that he did all this crap. Cathy had this smug look on her face, but the hammer was about to drop.

"I want a pregnancy test done now," Noah said. "I want proof, and since you don't want to take her to the doctor for proof, I'll call in a doctor to take the test here, but I want an answer before you start spouting lies. Cathy has told everyone that I'm the father of a child. I couldn't have had sex with her; I've been in a relationship with someone since I came here, and it's not her, who has had sex with two different guys in this office in the last month?"

"Noah has every right to have a test done when she tells everyone that he's the father," the Company lawyer said. "Plus, the fact that Cathy has been caught in more than one lie in the last month, he has a right to know now."

"Fine, I'll give a sample," Cathy said. I'll go to the restroom and give a sample.

"I want it stated that if she does this and it's positive, then Allen, Cathy, and Todd keep their jobs," Allen's lawyer said.

"Agreed," Noah said.

"This way, remove your jacket and follow me," Peggy said.

"I know where the bathroom is," Cathy barked.

"We are having you take the test in one of the offices with a single bathroom," Peggy said.

"Wait, you said I was going into the restroom," Cathy said, looking at her dad for help.

"We couldn't control people in the restroom, so we thought the office across the way would be better and private for you," Noah's lawyer said. "You're the one who told us that the restroom had too many people, and that's why you couldn't take the test. Now we have fixed that."

"Well, I'll take it in the restroom," Cathy said.

"No, we have made arrangements already," Noah's lawyer said.

"I think that is a good idea," Allen's lawyer said.

Cathy didn't know that we found the mason jar with the sample in it in the bathroom. Beth and Kim found it. We removed it, but we thought a different place was better. Noah hadn't known because I didn't have time to tell him.

"I think my daughter should do the sample where she wants to," Allen said.

"Fine, have the bathroom cleanout of people, and then she can give a sample," Noah said.

"Then give me ten minutes to get everyone out," Peggy said.

I sent a text to Beth telling her to check out the bathroom one more time, please, and I watched both ladies rush to the toilet. I owe them dinner when this is done, I thought. Peggy went and got everyone out, and then she followed Cathy in with one of Allen's attorneys. Then we started to hear yelling in the bathroom, and two security females ran in.

Then I got Beth's text: "We found another sample in a mason jar and took it out. We didn't find anymore."

Then Cathy came back with a sample, and she was furious, and I knew I owe the ladies lunches and dinner, all three of them. Cathy slammed the sample on the table. "They wouldn't let me out of the bathroom until I peed in a glass!"

"That is what you were going to do?" I spoke. Noah saw the smirk on my face and knew I had done something, and it pissed Cathy off. I winked, and Noah knew I was up to something.

They started doing the test, and two of the tests came up not pregnant. "I think Cathy should be able to do the test at the doctor's office," Allen said.

I texted Beth to bring in the samples they found. And Beth was at the door and handled the pieces to me.

"We found these in the female restroom, and I bet they will come up positive," I said.

"What are you talking about?" Allen's lawyer began. "Cathy was in this room the whole time."

"Well, when I went to use the restroom, I found this mason jar behind the toilet and thought it was odd. So, I had Security come in and take fingerprints for me. They will bring me the results," I said.

Right on time there was a knock on the door. Security brought the results of the prints finished the test on the mason jar. Then I handed the letter with the information to the lawyer, with a copy to Noah, "Can you get me, Tara Martin?" Noah asked.

"Yes, sir," Peggy said and left the room.

"The test shows that Todd and Tara's fingerprints are on both mason jars," The lawyer said.

"Well, that is that," Noah's lawyer said.

"I need to go to my office and get my stuff," Allen said.

"That won't be necessary," Noah said. "You're all packed up. All your meetings will be by me now. All your accounts are being given to other people; we called them all."

I watched Noah open the door as Peggy came back with Tara Martin, "Security, please escort them out, and Peggy, can you follow them make sure they get their boxes. When there out, send an email informing them they don't work here anymore and are not allowed in the building."

"I want to hear what she says," one of Allen's lawyers said.

"Fine with me," Noah said. "Tara, you get one chance to tell us how the mason jars with a sample in them got into the restroom with your fingerprints on them?"

"I'm pregnant, and Todd is the father, he told me to fill the jars with my pee and put them in the bathroom," Tara said.

"Who got you the jars," Noah asked.

"Todd and his dad," Tara said. "What's the big deal?" "Tara, you can go back to work now," Noah said.

"Why are you keeping her," Cathy demanded.

"Because she didn't lie to me," Noah said. "Goodbye, Allen." And Noah walked to his office.

"I want to make sure I got everything from my office that's mine," Allen stated.

"Your assistant did it all for you," Peggy said.

"Then I want to talk to my assistant before I go," Allen said.

"She will meet you at the front door," Peggy said.

I watched them leave and went to my old office to make sure everything was out of it. I checked the desk and the files, and it looked like Beth did a great job. As I was in there, I started thinking that maybe Allen's assistant didn't get everything. I don't know why but I went to his office. Kim was with me like she knew what I was thinking. "Are you thinking what I'm thinking?" Kim asked.

"That Allen had a secret something in his office," I said. We fist-bumped and started walking faster. My cell rang, and I answered it.

"Where did you go?" Noah asked.

"We are going to Allen's office to see if there anything else that needs to be looked at?" I spoke. "Kim is with me."

"There is a wall safe in that office," Noah said. "I'll be right up."

When we opened the door and saw Misty trying to open

Allen's safe, she didn't look like she was happy to be doing it.

"Here, Avery, I'll pack my bags and leave through HR," Misty said.

"Did you get fired?" I asked.

"I thought that's why you're here," Misty stated.

"No, we are here to get what in the safe," I said. "Is there anything else Allen told you to get?"

"Yes, these and the stuff from the other wall safe, it's a date calendar, I think looking at it," Misty said, pointing at the paper. "Look, Allen said you were going to fire me and if I can bring this stuff to him that he pays me ten grand. I have a child to take care of, and I need this job."

"How about this..." I started when Noah walked in. I explained what we walked in on and that she wanted to keep her job.

"You can be Doug's new assistant at the same pay and tell us everything that went on in this office," Noah began. "To make it even better, I'll throw in the ten grand. You're going to have to spend a couple of days with Avery showing her everything he did and how he operated behind closes doors."

"You don't have to give me the bonus. I'm only glad not to be working for Allen anymore," Misty said. "Doug is an amazing guy. I would love to work with him."

I turned the safe combination one more time, and it popped open. There was a bundle of cash in there and four files. "Where is the other safe?"

"Over here," and Misty pulled the picture so you could see it.

"Send Allen a message and tell him you were caught, and then block him off your cell," Noah said.

"I don't know how to do that," Misty said and just handed her cell to Noah. I found this interesting on many levels, but hought I'd worry about it later.

I opened the second one and found a file on ten people, and even one on Noah and me. I grabbed everything and found a book. When I opened it, there was money.

"You're a good worker, so you have a choice you can work with the person taking over my job, or Doug," I told her "Can I wait to see who gets the job?" Misty asked.

"Sure, it will take a couple of days. I want you to sit down with Kim and Beth and tell them everything you know. I mean all of it, and Kim and Beth can fill me in."

"So, you are the new boss?" Misty stated.

"Yep, and I'm bringing Beth with me," I said. "Kim, I want as detailed as you can get, and I want a copy to Noah, Peggy, and me."

We checked everything out, and I had the assistants check Todd's area too. I know I was crazy, but I wanted this all taken care of tonight. I was thumbing through the file that had my name, there were pictures, but they weren't me. They were Ben with Sophia coming out of a doctor's office. Then I realized he had Ben followed. I turned to the next page, and it was a picture of a computer screen that had Sophia's name and a positive pregnancy test. I stopped and was shocked by what I was seeing. "Everything, all right?" Kim asked, making Noah stop. "Avery, your pale as a ghost. What did you see?" Noah was at my side in a second; I didn't even see him move.

"Noah, you still love me, right?" Kim started taking the files from me, and I let her.

"What's the matter Avery?" Noah said.

Everything was going cold, started with my feet and up to my legs it just washed over me. "You don't love me" was the last thing I said before everything went black.

I woke to hear Noah yelling, and I was on Noah's office floor. How did I get there? "You were going to tell us tonight that Sophia is pregnant. Why didn't you tell us this a week ago instead of Avery finding out this way."

"Avery," Beth said, and I turned to look at her. "Honey, you're very dehydrated, and they put in an IV. I'm so glad you are awake."

"Avery," Noah said and came over to me. There were two people doing things to me that were starting to scare me. "Avery, I love you...never think I don't love you." I tried to move, but this one guy kept telling me to lay still.

"Ben's marrying Sophia," I said.

"I don't know what's going on, but I'm not ever leaving you," Noah said.

"Okay," I said with a forced half smile just as a man pulled up part of my shirt and put stuff on it.

"What are you doing?" I asked.

"They're checking the baby," Noah said. Then the room heard the heartbeat and everything in the room got very quiet. I looked at the portable laptop, and the tech turned it. I saw a little peanut where the man was pointing.

"There is your baby, safe and sound," he said.

"There's my peanut," I said, and Noah kissed my forehead. Another man sat next to me, a doctor I'm guessing, I didn't know, and I didn't care. I had my peanut, and whatever happened, I'd be there for this baby no matter what.

I didn't go to the hospital, but I did have an appointment in the morning, we delayed the trip for two more days. The doctor said I had a stressful day and would have to take it easy for the rest of the night, and if I was back to normal, I could come to work and do light work. I would have to have another ultrasound tomorrow to make sure everything was okay. Plus, blood work and so on. Noah was going no matter what happened tonight or tomorrow.

Ben was stuck until his flight time, and all Noah told him was I had passed out after seeing the file. When we got home, Noah brought me in first, then got the boxes with the files we had to go through. I told him I could lay on the couch and read, which made him happy, but we ended up on the bed instead because it had more room. I started going through the files and found out that Allen had been having a private investigator following us around. Noah found the name and called them. I didn't hear the conversation, but he's sending a lawyer there tomorrow.

I took the five-page report and started reading it. Everything was normal until I found the stuff on Ben and Sophie. It's instructed the P.I. to start with Avery's soon-be husband, who may be having an affair, and now she's pregnant. But what he found was a paid amount that Sophia had paid to a doctor to say she was pregnant when she wasn't. I showed it to Noah, and he relaxed some, but was still pissed. "Ben has no idea, and Ben has no idea you're the one who is pregnant."

"Let's see if he leaves me for her first," I said. "Then I'll have my answer."

We found out that Allen was blackmailing Sophia to keep the secret. That's where the money came from. We found files on all upper management people. Noah ordered chicken noodle soup and bread. They also added some grilled cheese sandwiches and more potato skins for all of us. Instead of meeting Ben at the airport, we waited for him to come home. He knew I knew. We sat at the table and had just started eating when Ben stepped thought the door. He took his coat off and came to the table and sat down. His food was in front of him, but he leaned back, grabbed a bottle of whiskey off the counter, poured himself a glass, and downed it before he started.

"Sophia said she was trying to get ahold of you because she had something important to tell you. So, I met her for lunch in town four weeks ago. She told me she was pregnant. I knew you wouldn't believe her, and so I went to her doctor's appointment, and she is with child," Ben said like he was just putting it out there. "Since you and she have never had a child, she said it has to be mine."

"So, you're going to marry her and forget all about me," I said.

"I don't know what I'm going to do," Ben stated. "I've been thinking about it, and I thought Noah could marry her again, and now he has his family he wants."

"I'm not marrying her," Noah said. "Over my dead body."

"You know, in this lifestyle, this could happen," Ben said.

"Yes, but what you want to do is replace me for her because she is pregnant," I said. "Was that the plan to replace me now that she can have kids?"

"I wish she weren't pregnant," Ben said. "I want to marry you."

"Noah can marry me, and you can have Sophia. That is the only reason I can think of that you didn't tell us," I said. I grabbed the grilled cheese and started eating it. It tasted so good. I was mad, furious but this grilled cheese was making me happy.

"So, what is your plan since both of you have knocked up not one but two women," I said. "Each of you marries one and hope the DNA for that child is in the right woman."

"I don't want to marry her, but we have a responsibility to the child," Ben said. Not even listening to what I just said, but Noah did.

"Fine, I'll marry Avery, and you can marry Sophia, and that way, both children will have a father. We will just not know which father," Noah said.

I got up, got the papers, highlighted the part about pregnancy, and handed them to Ben. Then sat back down, "If you want to marry Sophia after reading this, then you can have her take my spot for our wedding."

"I don't understand why you didn't tell me before now," Noah said. "If you had told me four weeks ago, we could have sat calmly and found a way. Remember, that's how Sophia messed us up the first time. BTW I was tested. I can have children without a problem. It was Sophia who would never get tested."

I grabbed some more potato skins and started eating them. "Peanut is craving some weird stuff."

"Sophia is not pregnant. She was being blackmailed by Allen when he had a private detective following me," I said.

"You're getting the security team tomorrow," Ben said.

"No, I'm not, I'm not married to you yet," I said. "Noah, can you order some more potato skins, like four, maybe five orders?"

"Sure, anything you and peanut want you will get," Noah said. He punched in a text for the order while Ben was just looking at us both like we were crazy.

My cell had a text, and I read it. "The ultrasound has to be forty-five minutes later," I set my phone down and looked from one potential husband to the other. "Are you okay with going to the hospital with me?" I asked them both.

"You have more tests. I thought you had a virus, or something. Is it worse?" Ben asked, looking at me in horror.

"Nothing that can't be fixed in six and half months," I said. "Are you coming with me or not, Ben?"

"I think a security team for Ben is a good idea right now. Don't you think so, Noah?" I asked.

"I agree since he can't be trusted," Noah said.

"I'm going to rent a plane on Thursday. I still need to fly our team to that meeting," I said.

"Sure," Ben said, confused and unsure what was happening.

"I'm coming with you now that I have to replace Alan," Noah said. "I'll be your co-pilot."

I cleared my throat and basically made a proclamation. "We have agreed that Sophia is no longer in our lives. I will marry Ben if he still wants to, but we are having a commitment ceremony before the wedding. I want to be married to both of you even when one is a horse's ass. Let's see, and whatever I crave, you will get for me, and you will never say I'm fat even if I say it. When we decide to have kids next time, we will go on a break from the other people in our lives to know if the father of my child is Noah or you. We will have a list of who we can or can't sleep with written down since I can't play on the honeymoon the way I wanted to. You two still can. I want a daycare at work for age groups. I'll have our group put it together. Am I missing anything else?"

"I agree with all of it, but Ben is just sitting there," Noah smirked. Ben wasn't listening to anything we were talking about at all. "I have not slept with Sophie since we did everything on Christmas holiday. What about you, Ben?"

"I don't want to have kids for two years," Ben stated, not answering the question.

"Too late, you can't have your way," I said. "Do you agree with the rest?"

"I thought we agreed to wait on children," Ben said.

"Not when you are thinking of marrying Sophia because she said she was pregnant," I said. "We also need a bigger place after the wedding and honeymoon. We will start looking now because we have to have it before Christmas. November would be good,"

"Wait, everything you are saying is going too fast for me. I know you're pissed, but we had a plan. I don't understand why we have to be in a bigger house by November?"

"I told you everything already and why we need to be in a bigger house. If you don't want to marry me, tell me now so I can call my parents and tell them the wedding is off. Get this straight I'm marrying one of you in the next two weeks." I stood up and went to our bedroom.

"Is this her way of making me suffer for hiding something I knew would piss her off?" I heard Ben ask.

"Ben, you have had a long day, so have we, but you have heard everything, and you're still missing it," Noah said. "Be happy she still wants to marry you because I want to hit you in the face for meeting with my ex-wife."

Chapter Eleven

The following day, Ben made breakfast and made me a plate, and when I sat down and looked down at the eggs, I grabbed my mouth because my stomach decided I wasn't going to eat them or see them. I ran to the bathroom and started throwing up. I heard the door, and someone put a cool washcloth on the neck. "What happened?" Noah asked.

"There are eggs on my plate, and Peanut doesn't like them," I said.

I returned to the room, and Ben was sitting at the table, "I guess you're still sick," Ben said. "I've been thinking, and I think we should check this out and make sure Sophia is not pregnant at all."

Noah grabbed my plate and replaced it with bacon and biscuits. "What is the plan?"

"She is four, almost five months along, she is telling you?" I asked.

"That's what she told me, and I want to know for sure before we block her from our lives," Ben said.

"You know she was lying," Noah said.

"Whatever you do, you are doing it together," I said.

"You want me to go in there with Noah and make her admit that she is not pregnant," Ben stated.

"Why don't you just set up an ultrasound today because you're both excited to see the baby, and that way, there are no tricks. Noah can get one fast if he calls the hospital, he has a friend there," I started. "You will both be there, and you can see if she has a baby in there or not." "That's a good idea," Noah said.

"Don't let her set it up," I said. "Don't give her a chance to find a way to say no. Noah can help with that." "Noah makes the appointment," Ben said.

"What will we do if she is pregnant?" I asked. "Who is marrying her?"

"I don't know, but one of us needs to," Ben said. "I'm talking about a child here."

"I won't live in this house or be with the man that marries her," I said.

"First, the appointment is an hour, Avery. Second, I won't be marrying Sophia, so if Ben wants to marry her, I will marry you, as we discussed it before," Noah said.

"Since you're both going to be there for Sophia, then you both will be there for me?" I asked.

"I have to move things around, but I'll make it work," Noah said. "What about you, Ben?"

"I can do an hour, but I don't know if I can do two?" Ben said.

"Make it work, Ben," Noah said. "Or I'll meet with Sophia, and you can meet us at Avery's appointment."

"I'll make it work. I want to see that Sophia is not pregnant and that you're okay Avery," Ben said.

"How many files did you go through last night," Noah asked.

"Three. I thought I would review the others before the appointment. Peggy is right about the three so far and is sending over the videos today. Let's let it all go and fire the people on Friday. That way, we have more time to look over the other two and anything in the videos, too, so we can have one bad day instead of two or three," I stated.

"Good idea. I think this will work out. What else did you want to do, or were you joking yesterday?" Noah asked.

I looked over, and Ben was on the cell with Sophia. I knew he was by the way he was standing. I turned around and looked at Noah. "I have ideas, and with Peanut on the way, I would like to have a daycare put in and have it by age, not just one. I was thinking of three rooms preschool, middle age, and maybe a video room for the kids. That way, if the kids must come in, they are not crazy. I want to put a gym in so all employees can go. Plus, a couple of other things," I said. "My office is big enough to have a playpen in there for Peanut."

"What made you think of all this," Noah asked.

"On Saturdays, we have employees freaking out about daycare, and new moms are quitting because of daycare costs," I began. "We would have better production if people felt their kids were safe."

"So, you want to head it up," Noah asked.

"Really!!" I jumped out of the chair into Noah's arms. "I love you."

"Love you too," Noah said, and Ben came in and looked at us both.

"What is going on?" Ben asked.

"Remember when we talked about what I would do differently, or I start my own business," I said.

"Yes, but after Noah and we came together, I thought you forgot about that. I thought that way you could come with me. That's why we taught you to be a pilot," Ben said.

"We have to get going if we are going to have Sophia at the hospital in time," Noah said. "Avery, are you coming or going to meet us there?"

"I think meeting you there would be better," I stated. "I don't want to wait an hour for my appointment."

As the men headed out the door, "Why is Avery seeing the doctor?" Ben said.

"She told you why you don't remember last night," Noah said. And that's all I heard as they were out of earshot.

Chapter Twelve

Sophie has Ben so messed up right now. I sat at the table and started going through the files I needed to get done.

I called Beth and made sure everything was great at the office. The investigator was in the office and brought more stuff to Ben's office, and I asked for it to be sent to me. I got it as I was sitting in the waiting room for my appointment when I saw even more pictures of Ben and Sophie, and they went back four weeks; they were meeting all the time. There were so many pictures of Ben and Sophie, some in front of a hotel, coming out of a hotel room together, and some even kissing outside.

How much has he hidden from us? I thought as my name was called. I saw Noah come up, and I didn't see Ben. "Where's Ben?"

"First lets, get you in here, and we can talk," Noah said. As they had me change, I went to the table and sat down. Noah had his head down and Couldn't stop playing with his fingers.

"What's up?" I asked.

"Sophie is pregnant, and she is less than three weeks," Noah said.

"Great, that means Ben, and you are not the father," I said.

"Where is Ben?"

"Talking to Sophie," Noah said.

"Why isn't he here?" I asked. Then I stopped and remembered all the new files I had seen. Ben slept with Sophie again.

That was all I could think of.

"Hi, I'm Sara. Do you want a DVD of the baby?"

"Yes, please, we both said," as she had me pull open my gown and put the jelly on my stomach. I had a tear fall. Ben wasn't coming in, and I knew it. He gave it all up for Sophie. Sara started moving the wand around, and the heartbeat was loud and clear, bringing me back to why I was here. They took many pictures of Peanut, and then I found out that I was twelve weeks along. But the baby looked perfect. I was crying now for a different reason. After all the tests were done and I got a prescription for a prenatal vitamin, I was allowed to go home, and Noah came with me.

"How is the office going?" I asked.

"Kim is calling me and asking us questions. I told her we would not be in today. I told her the rest of everything went great. I was also told you asked for the rest of Ben's file."

"Yes, and I looked it over before the appointment," I told him as we were leaving. "You won't like it Ben has been lying for over a month. Do you think his family knows?"

"No, because Tiffany would kill him," Noah said. I looked at my cell as Noah drove and then backed up at him.

"Sophie is trying to get ahold of you again," I said. "Kim knows it will upset you, so she sent it to me. Sophie wants to meet with you."

"No way in hell will I meet up with her again," Noah said. "This reminds me of the time that Sophie did the same thing to me to get me to marry her."

"She didn't," I said.

"She did."

"I'm doing the same thing," I said.

"No, we were planning on marrying you before we knew you were with a child," Noah quickly pointed out.

Then I looked down and saw another text with a video attached. I opened it and saw Sophie having sex with Alan. "Is Alan in your group of people you had sex with?"

"No," Noah said. "I kept that out of my company. We did business with people but not someone I work with every day. But I had been with you before I knew you worked for me."

"I have a video here of Sophie having sex with Alan, and it looks like two different times, one dated four weeks ago, and the other was a week ago," I said.

"Sophie slept with everyone, but I was told who I could sleep with," Noah said.

"Ben and I agreed that we had to ask first before we slept with someone. After the Sophie thing," I said.

"Do you want to order lunch for us, and we can go over more files, and the rest of the files from that detective," Noah said.

"I think I need to move out of Ben's place," I said.

"I have a place closer to the office, and we can live there. It has five rooms, so big enough for a baby and us," Noah said.

"Why didn't you tell us about it before?"

"Sophie and I used it when I had worked up here, but I want to change it or sell it," Noah said. "I kept it after the divorce because Sophie didn't like it here. She said it wasn't her taste. I had it done more for me when I needed it for guests or family."

"Could we stay there tonight?" I asked. "Should I just get a hotel room?"

"Where you go, I go. If you want to stay at my house, let me call the maid and get it ready," Noah said.

"Well, let's get it done before we meet with Ben just in case," I said.

I got on my cell and ordered lunch for the two of us, and then Noah stopped by the office to pick up some more things. I showed the pictures of Peanut to Kim and Beth, they were happy.

We got back into the car and went to Ben's place. I was disconnecting myself from all this. Then Ben called Noah. I heard it all from the car but didn't say a word. "We need to talk about Sophie," Ben said.

"I'm not the father, and she's only three weeks along, not the four months she told us," Noah said.

"You haven't been with her in four weeks," Ben asked.

"No, I've been with Avery, and Tiffany, and you know that."

"Avery has rules about who we are with, and I've kept them," Noah said. I looked at Noah. He has been with Ben too. I thought they had, but they never said anything.

"Sophie wants us all together to talk about this," Ben stated.

"What about Avery?"

"She knows a child is involved and that we need to think of Sophie's child," Ben said.

"Did you sleep with Sophie after Avery told you not to?" Noah asked.

"Yes, I slept with her one night, and I just knew it was wrong, but I messed up, and now I'm in trouble," Ben said.

"Avery is pregnant, and you're not caring for the child she is carrying," Noah said.

"Avery's, not pregnant," Ben said.

"Yes, she is. Three months along. That's what the appointment was for, and you missed it," Noah said.

"Wait, Avery's, pregnant too," Ben stated.

"Yes, she told you last night, and she is calling the baby Peanut," Noah said. "Please explain why Sophie's baby is more important than Avery's."

"I was so worried about Sophie I didn't hear what we were talking about," Ben said.

"Avery's baby has more of a chance to be yours than Sophie's baby could be," Noah began. "That's why I said if you don't marry Avery, I will."

"Why can't you marry Sophie? She needs you too," Ben stated. "That way, we can all be together." I shook my head no.

"Avery will not go with that after what she did," Noah said. "I'm meeting Avery at home for lunch this would be a good time to talk to her. She's mad you missed the appointment."

"Well Avery will get over it. She loves me and will understand we are in the lifestyle," Ben said.

I don't think, so I mouthed I was getting pissed by the minute, and then I looked at my cell phone and knew I wouldn't be staying at Ben's place tonight.

"Being in the lifestyle still means putting the main woman in your life first, not a weekend fun time girl," Noah said. I started texting Tiffany and telling her what just happened. I needed a woman's advice, and Tiffany would give it to me. After I texted the whole story, I waited for Tiffany to text back. "Avery and I are getting married in two weeks," Ben stated.

"Not if you want Sophie in your life, you won't," Noah said.

Chapter Thirteen

I put the crash behind me and instead focused on the wedding that suddenly became two weeks away. I talked to Tiffany daily about arrangements and her "to-do" list. Things were coming together. Now they have all fallen apart. I can't believe Ben slept with that bitch so many times, it was more than once. He lied so much in the last couple of weeks.

It's normal for him now.

It explains why Ben had been possessive of me, not wanting to share me because he knew when I found out it was over with him, but he thought Noah would follow him. He thought he would lose me but not Noah. Ben thought Noah loved him enough to give up me even after Sophie did so much damage to Noah. "Ben thought he lost me, but not you," I stated, sitting in the car as we drove.

"What are you talking about?" Noah said.

"Ben knew I would never agree to Sophie. That's why he acted like I would leave him soon. I thought he was acting up because of the plane crash, you know he almost lost me, but that wasn't it. It was the first time he had to deal with the fact that I could be gone soon," I took a deep breath "Now that Sophie is with child Ben thinks that you would go with Sophie and him and leave me behind. That I would dismiss everything that she done to me because she pregnant."

We arrived home and I immediately located my suitcase. I love Ben, but I will never be with him and Sophie. Never. Noah was in the other room finding his suitcase and packing. As I was picking out my clothes. The thought of Ben sleeping with Sophie, and I plagued my mind. I need to be tested for sexual transmitted diseases now. I ran to the bathroom to throw up. I felt sick and it had nothing to do with Peanut.

"Are you okay?" Noah asked, coming into the bathroom, pulling my hair back and applying a cold cloth to my neck.

"It's not the baby, it's the idea that Ben has been sleeping with us both," I said.

"I was thinking the same thing with Ben and me. He knew Sophie made my life hell," Noah began. "I thought the three of us would be happy, I guess Ben didn't feel that way."

"I thought the same thing," I said, sitting back against the wall, taking the wet cloth from my neck, and wiping my face before speaking again. "I texted Tiffany and told her everything."

"I bet she's pissed right now," Noah said.

"I told her you wanted to marry me."

"How do you feel about that?"

"When you came to live with us, it felt right. I thought that everything worked out great and we were a happy family. We have been together for over three months as one happy group, but now we find out that it was just a lie. Was he planning on marrying me and then have her on the side?"

Chapter Fourteen

"No, Sophie would never allow that. She has wanted Ben all her life but also have group sex. I wanted to give it all up and make it just another couple so we could still have fun sometimes," Noah said bending down and sitting next to me.

"What do you want now?" I asked.

"I want you to have kids with you but if you want to leave the lifestyle, I'm okay with that. If you want to stay in the lifestyle. I'm good with that too.

"Noah, right now, I don't know what I want except for you," Taking a deep breath, I just don't understand why Ben did this. I thought he loved me too."

There was a knock on the door, and Noah got up and held out his hand for me to stand. He kissed my cheek before I went to brush my teeth. When I came out of the bathroom, Sophie was sitting on the couch, and I watched Noah pull out the ordered food. I went over, took a sandwich, and sat down next to him. "What is she doing here?" Sophie began. "You better start packing. I'm moving in tonight and out of Noah's place. We three are going to be one happy family."

"We will leave as soon as Ben gets here," Noah said.

Sophie's eyes narrowed at Noah "You're not leaving Ben said you were staying. Ben and I are getting married because of the baby, and then we were having a private ceremony after." "We are staying at the hotel tonight," I stated.

"I had the keys changed. I have someone picking up Sophie's stuff and I had a new bed ordered that will be delivered by this afternoon," Noah whispered to me.

"You're the best," I whispered back.

"What are you two talking about?" Sophie asked.

"How long have you and Ben been dating," I asked.

"Five weeks. We been in touch since Noah moved in, and I was with him when he got that call about your flying accident. I wish you had crashed the plane. That way, things would have been easier you know," Sophie said.

"I can't believe you said that," Noah yelled.

"Will you give it up," Sophie whined. "Ben said you're staying with us so stop trying to be the wrong person. Just help Avery pack her things and when Ben gets here it will be fast."

"Are you done Avery," Noah asked me, then softly said. "Turn on your video and set it up before you start packing." "Yes, I'll go pack my bags," I said.

"I'll take the office work down to the car and I'll be right back," Noah began looking at Sophie. "Don't talk to her or go near her or I will make sure you will pay for it." "I'll stay right on this couch," Sophie stated.

I heard Noah packing all the stuff up. He took another look at Sophie, "Don't go near her or touch her, your pregnant you have to be careful." He practically ran out the door closing it

Chapter Fourteen

loudly.

Sophie came through the door a couple of minutes later watching me before she said "Ben and Noah are lovers and Noah loves me so that leaves you out in the cold. I hope there no hard feelings I just kept on packing, not saying a word. "Look bitch" pulling me around and slapping me. "Ben and Noah are mine; they have always been mine and will always be mine. You got the men back together but it's me they really want."

"I think you have your facts wrong," I said. I closed the suitcase and grabbed another suitcase and just started taking everything out of the closet. "Ben is going to lose a lot today I hope your enough."

"Bitch, it is you who will lose it all," Sophie said.

Part of me wanted to tell her off, the other part wanted to bitch slap her. I held my temper and then she went into Ben's bathroom and started throwing my makeup and then grabbed my shampoo and poured it into my suitcase. The door swung open, and Noah and Ben came in. "If I had my way, I'd hire someone to kill you, but since Ben and Noah are on my side, I'll let you live."

"Sophie, I told you to stay away from her," Noah said. "Avery, are you okay?"

"Yes, she threatened me and then poured shampoo into my suitcase," I said, looking at Ben. "Sophie's baby is more important than mine is?"

"I didn't know, Avery," Ben said.

"She's lying, she's not pregnant," Sophie laughed.

"Avery is three months along," Noah said. "I saw the ultrasound and if Ben had taken time to go to Avery's appointment, he would have seen it too."

Noah turned his attention to Ben "Well Ben what did you think was going to happen when all this came out?"

"You're three months along? You were pregnant when you crashed the plane," Ben realized. "When did you find out?"

"When she passed out at work," Noah said.

"You didn't want to marry me?" I asked.

"Yes, I still want to, but Sophie is pregnant and since she hasn't been with anyone else it has to be mine," Ben said.

"You are so stupid to think that Sophie didn't sleep with anyone else," Noah scoffed.

"What are you talking about?" Ben began. "We each need to marry one of them."

Noah handed Ben the investigation report, and ben dropped to the bed and started reading. I closed my suitcase and grabbed my gym bag and my cell phone and stopped the recording and put it in my pocket.

"Ben, we had rules about who we could be with and who was a hard limit. Why did you break it?" I asked. "I followed your rules but you couldn't follow the one rule I had."

"Because he loves me, and no hard limit would keep him away from me," Sophie smugly.

"Is that all of it?" Ben asked.

"There's video and more," Noah said. "I can't believe you thought I would go along with this."

"Noah, are you ready to go?" I asked.

"You made your choice, you don't want to marry me, and after you've been with Sophie, I will never be with you again," I took my ring off and handed it to Sophie "This is yours now."

"Wait, what are you doing?" Ben asked again.

"I had one hard limit, and it was Sophie, you knew it and still slept with her. I know who the possible fathers are and so do you, but do you know everyone Sophie has been with?" There was a tense silence, no one said a word, so I kept talking "I'm getting married in two weeks and I'm three months pregnant and you couldn't take the time to come to my doctor's appointment because of Sophie." "'I still want to marry you," Ben said.

"If you loved me, you would have never been with her!" I shouted.

"I will pick up all the costs of the wedding," Noah said. "I know Sophie wants to plan her own wedding to you."

"As you said before, if your married in and in the lifestyle the father is the husband not the friends with benefits," I said.

"We are getting married," Ben said again like he couldn't understand what was happening right now.

"No we are not, I was planning on marrying both of you but now I'm only marrying Noah," I began. "Now you can have your Sophie and I'll have someone who loves and wants me.

"Since we were in college you let Sophie run over your life," Noah said. "When she told us she was pregnant, you didn't want to be a father and I stepped up. Back then I wanted you both, but then you blamed me for taking Sophie. I didn't take Sophie away from you. You did that yourself." Noah took a deep breath and took the bags out of the room and down to the car, as I looked for a couple more things. He came back faster than I thought he would and went to his room. I followed him in. He had tears in his eyes.

"Noah, stop for a minute and breath," I whispered.

"I have to get out of this apartment before I do something I will regret," Noah said.

I knew Noah loved Ben very much, but I don't think Ben knew how much. I had to ask the question that was on my mind right now. Did Noah love me, or did he want to stay with him and Sophie? I had to find out before I left. I wanted both my men happy and if that meant Noah staying, I would be hurt, but I would know. "Noah, do you want to stay with them?" I asked.

"Avery, I love you, at first it was to be with Ben but after that plane crash, I knew I loved you so much and if you hadn't made it I would have taken my life to be with you," Noah began still packing, but shaking too. "Ben knew Sophie was my hard limit too. My heart is breaking but for what could have been.

You're still going to marry me, right?" "Yes," I whispered and Noah kissed me.

"Let's get Peanut to my place and tomorrow we will look for a new house and start changing the wedding arrangements," Noah said holding out his hand. I looked down and then put my hand in his. "First thing we are doing is getting you an engagement ring."

"Okay," I said. "If that will make you happy?"

"It would," Noah said as we left the room. We heard Sophie and Ben arguing in the front room and stopped when they heard us.

"We need to talk about this?" Ben said.

"No, you have made your choice and I'm making mine," Noah said, opening the door. "Sophie, if I find you in my offices again, I will arrest you."

"I'm getting a restraining order tomorrow on Sophie," I said as I walked out the door.

"What did you do to Avery?" Ben asked.

Chapter Fifteen

We didn't say a word going down the stairs, but once we got outside and put everything in the car, Noah spoke up. "Did you video tape Sophie?"

"Yes," I pulled out my phone, found the video and then handed it over to Noah. Noah watched it then handled back the cell. "Don't delete it. I have a plan."

"Okay," I said quietly still trying to hold my feelings in until we got to Noah's place, but one tear fell, and Noah wiped it away. "I thought he loved us."

Noah looked at me "I thought he loved us too." He looked out the window and just sat there. "We are going to have to fire everyone involved tomorrow," Noah said.

"I was thinking the same thing," I said.

"Well let's get you that ring," Noah smiled as he said it.

"We can do the ring tomorrow," I said.

"Have you changed your mind?" Noah asked starting the car.

"No, we both have had our hearts broken..."

"That's why we need to do it now, "so we have something to be happy about," Noah offered.

"Where are we going?" I asked as we were hitting a stop light. So where is this ring at?"

"My office."

"How long have you had it?"

"One month after I moved here," Noah stated looking at me for a minute and then back to the street. I was about to comment when my cell started going off.

"It's Tiffany," I said.

"Answer it."

"Hi Tiffany."

"My bastard of a brother did that to you. I'm going to kill him, and with Sophie of all people. Please tell me that Noah didn't stay with them?" Tiffany started.

"Noah wants to marry me. You should know that Sophie is pregnant," I stated.

"Wasn't Sophie your hard limit?" Tiffany asked.

"Yes! Thank you for knowing my hard limit since your brother acted like he didn't know," I began "I have something to tell you. I'm three months pregnant myself."

"My bastard of a brother left you three months pregnant to marry Sophie?" Tiffany asked.

"Yes."

"When I was there planning the wedding, he was crazy about having time alone with you. What happened?"

"Ben was sleeping with Sophie for the last month, and I think he knew when I found out that our life together would be over. He thought that Noah would stay with them, and everyone would leave me," I said.

"I'll keep you over my brother right now. So, are you still getting married in two weeks?" Tiffany asked.

I looked over at Noah "We are getting married in two weeks. Just something will need to be changed," Noah said.

"Yes, we are getting married," I repeated. "There are some-things that will need to change."

"We still coming to the honeymoon?" Tiffany asked with gusto.

"Yes, we are still doing that," I said.

"I'm getting off the cell so I can yell at my brother," Tiffany stated. "I have to move somethings around; I'll try to be on a plane as soon as I can."

"Can't wait to see you, and have fun yelling at Ben. I'm still in shock but I know we will have it out," I said and hung up. Noah drove under the building, into his parking spot, but I wasn't sure if he wanted me to come with him or not. Then he came around and opened my door. and held out his hand for me. I took it and got out of the car.

Still holding my hand, he took me up to his office, turned on the light and went to his desk, took out a key and unlocked it. I sat in a chair after everything I've been thinking about today, I started feeling dizzy and sat down quite fast. This did not go unnoticed by Noah, who was around his desk really fast making sure I was okay.

"What's wrong?" Noah asked.

"It's been a long day, and I'm dizzy," I said.

"It's been a hard day," Noah said on his knees before me. "Ever since the first time I met you I wanted to be with you, and then when I was, I didn't want to let you go. Ben had you first, but I would share you to have you. Will you marry me and make me the happiest man in the world?"

"Yes. I love you, but please don't do what Ben did to me," I said.

"Never," Noah said and opened the box with three rings.

"I bought you a ring," I said. Looking at the rings I knew none of them were the one he bought before because, Ben and Noah had gotten the same design but different stones in the ring. The plan was when I got the rings. I would have the same stones put into their rings. This design is not the same. I saw these rings in the glass window at Tiffany's on a business trip with Noah. There in the little box was a platinum princess-cut blue diamond that had six or seven karats. The one I looked at had three karats. The bands were the same. 'This is not the original ring you got me."

"How do you know?" Noah asked. "Never mind, this is for new beginnings."

"When did you get this?" I asked.

"On that business trip we were on, and you saw it. The only problem with the ring was it needed a couple more karats. I wanted to get it for you when you saw it, but Ben would be upset. At the time, I was keeping the peace. I thought I'd give it to you later in our marriage or anniversary."

"I love it and you. What else have you bought me that you're hiding?" I asked.

"You will have to wait and find out," Noah said, kissing me.

There was a knock on the door and Peggy, Beth, and Kim came in. "What is the emergency?"

Chapter Sixteen

"Sophie has been coming and going around this building and now she threatened to kill Avery," Noah said.

"Sir, do you have proof?" Peggy asked.

Kim and Beth looked scared on hearing what Noah had said. I took my cell out and found the video and handed it to Beth who gave it to Peggy, and she hit play while all three of them watched. I walked to the door "Where are you going?" Noah asked.

"Get some water, I'll be right back," I said and left the room. I needed a chance to breathe so I went to the break room and grabbed my glass and got some water. I left the light off, I have done this more than once, so I knew where everything was at. I sat in a chair and looked down at the bracelet I was wearing and ripped it off my arm. Ben had given it to me. The one thing I did was take back the photo album I gave Ben for Christmas. I knew where he kept it. In his suitcase he takes out for trips. I wonder how long it will be before he realized I took it.

"Are you alright," Beth asked.

"Yes, just thinking about when everything started feeling off. I want to say four weeks ago but I know it was longer. He started acting like he was scared of losing me. He was buying me stuff more this month than he ever did. That bracelet, earrings, flowers, candy, a gift card..."

"Ben sends you flowers three times a month since you started dating, but this last month it's been more like eight or nine times. I'd have to check. He sent you gift cards on some of them. I took them off the flowers and put them in your desk drawer," Beth said.

"I thought there was only one."

"You had flowers delivered to you today, I didn't check," for a card. Do you want me to go get it?"

"Why don't we both look, and I'll look at the other gift cards," I said and we got up and headed over to my new office. I saw the new flowers and went to open the card.

Avery
I know last night was hard for you to hear.
I love you and we can make this work.
Sophie said she can work on all of us living together.
Think about it. Noah wants this too. Ben

I walked through the door connecting to Noah's office, and four more people were in the room. "What's going on?"

"After we saw Sophie in the building, I had extra video cams installed and asked anyone in security if they wanted more hours, mostly our part-time workers, and make them full-time. Peggy picked whom she wanted. Anyway, two men got into the building and are being held in the security area," Noah said.

"We sent the video of Sophie and you to the police. Noah wanted her arrested for threatening you because she can get a little crazy at times," Peggy stated. "Plus, we think Sophie is targeting you."

"Why?" I asked, handing the card to Noah to read.

"The men who came into the building were in your old office and wrote something on the walls," Peggy said.

I went to look "Avery stop!" Noah said. "The police don't want anyone in the room until pictures and everything is taken."

"Okay, so now what's going on?" I asked.

"Police are on their way and we are to stay here, part of my security is down stairs with the men and the detective is on his way," Peggy stated. "Beth, tell Noah what you told me on the way over here."

"Peggy asked me if I was seeing anything different in Avery's day," Beth started. "I told her that she been getting more deliveries than normal. Normally Ben sends her flowers three to four times a month. When he leaves town normally when his going on a business trip. This month been really different." "What has she gotten?" Noah asked.

"I don't read the notes, unless Avery talks to me about it," Beth said.

"Okay, this month has been different but with the wedding I thought it was normal," I began. "I got jewelry, flowers, gift cards."

"Did you keep the notes," Noah asked.

"Yes, I have a drawer just for the notes and so on, the earrings Ben got me for the wedding is in there and I keep all my notes.

I have the note and coffee card you got me. I keep forgetting to take it home with me. The Bracelet I got this month is in the breakroom I took it off after everything."

"I forgot. You got another small gift box when we were moving your office. I put it in the drawer to keep it safe," Beth said.

"Did it come with the flowers," I asked.

"No, it was delivered on its own with a box of candy," Beth said. I saw this guy she called Brad but didn't know him.

"Beth, can you get it all and bring it to this room. Brad, can you get the bracelet from the breakroom," Peggy said.

"Noah, what's going on?" I asked.

"I'll explain everything in a minute, I'm still trying to understand," Noah said. Before taking out his cell and making a call.

"I need to know something. We will talk about that later, this is important, just answer the question. What did you send Avery this month?"

I'm trying to understand what is going on. That question was interesting. Beth came in with my drawer pulled out.

Noah was listening to Ben, but I still don't understand what's going on. I kept watching him. Noah has his no-bullshit face on right now and whatever Ben was telling him was not going over well. "Just tell me, I'm not in the mood for that conversation right now," Noah said. I just sat and watched him.

"Avery, why don't you sit down," Kim said. I just sat down and Kim brought me some orange juice. "You're looking a little pale." I took a drink but watched Noah talking to Ben. "I called the Detective I don't think you were the target."

I just realized that the men in my life were keeping something from me. Has Noah been lying to me too?

Noah got off the cell and Brad came in with the bracelet and showed something to Peggy. "Avery, this bracelet has a GPS tracker on it," Peggy said showing it to Noah.

"Is someone stalking me?" I whispered.

Chapter Seventeen

"Ben sent flowers three times and a gift card," Noah said. Peggy put plastic gloves on and started looking thought everything in the drawer. "That is Ben's writing and so is that one." This went on until they got to the gift cards with the notes. "I sent that one, and Ben sent that one."

I listened to what was going on around me without saying a word. Noah had told Ben he wasn't the target. What did that mean? When they got through with the gift cards, they opened the earrings. Peggy picked up the last two boxes that came in, one was a candy box with chocolates, and the other looks like jewelry. She didn't open them. "I'll let the Detective open theses," Peggy said.

My cell went off and it was Ben. I declined the call and then I got a text: Are you okay?

While everyone was around me only Beth and Kim seemed to be watching me. Noah had his all-business look that told me he was taking everything in. I trusted the men in my life, was that a mistake? "The police are here I need to go downstairs" Peggy said. It was after ten and I needed to know what was going on before the police started asking questions.

"Noah, what is going on?" I asked.

"Let's go into your office and talk," Noah said, as he helped me up and guided me through my office door, following close behind me. I sat on the couch as Noah sat next to me. I didn't say anything, I waited for him to start. "Ben was getting death threats," Noah said.

"Why didn't you tell me?" I asked.

"Ben didn't want me to tell you. See, first it was pictures from Christmas asking for money to keep the lifestyle a secret from the business world. Your name was brought up many times in the notes that were sent, but the Detective thought they were just going after Ben. Then the letters started getting more disturbing. We found out that the plane crash wasn't an accident. Someone messed with the landing gear. The Detective thought you were in the wrong place at the wrong time. He also thinks it could be someone from our lifestyle that is doing it."

"Why the lifestyle?" I asked.

"They seem to be sending pictures of anyone Ben has been with," Noah said.

"Has there been pictures of me?" I asked tentatively.

"Just one, the others were of other women with, "What if Avery found out?" printed on them. The apartment was safe, nothing came from there, but from his office, and other business trips. Then the messages started saying you can't marry Avery," Noah said.

"Did any of these pictures have Sophie in them?" I asked.

"I don't know, he never told me," Noah stated. Someone knocked on the door and Noah opened it.

"Avery, why didn't you open the envelopes," Peggy asked.

"Because Ben only writes on the envelopes, he never leaves me a card inside," I said. "I opened Noah's because he leaves notes."

"Thank you," and she walked out, and Noah closed the door. This reminded me about that movie I watched with the millionaire who was into BDSM. Well, I'm not going to be stupid like she was.

"You two didn't think I needed to know that someone was doing this? What do I look like, a weak woman or something?" I asked.

"It was all about Ben and him leaving you. I didn't know you were getting all these deliveries," Noah said. I sat there and thought about the private investigator who was following us all around. Had my ex-boss been doing all this or is it simply two different things happening at once. "Avery, say something?"

"Have Peggy give all that stuff from the private investigator, and the names of all the people we plan to fire tomorrow to the detective. There may be a connection," I said.

"I never thought of that," Noah said.

"That is why you should have told me when all this started, I could have had the plane checked out before I left," I said, "We did, well Ben did while you were in that meeting," Noah said. "I'm just glad we had all your things moved out before the office was vandalized. We had a temp in there helping with back-up work."

"Anything else you need to tell me?" I asked.

"I thought I knew everything, but it looks like Ben wasn't telling me everything," Noah admitted.

"Don't do this again do you understand me. I want an honest relationship, I don't care how bad it is, you will tell me from now on," I demanded. "Did you go into my office?"

"No, only two people from night security have, then the room was locked down for the Detective," Noah said. "Before you ask, I have not received any mail or anything from work."

"Well, that's good," I began and then looked up at him "What did you mean, he may not be the target?"

"Well, when this all started, I had said that someone was trying to get you out of Ben's life," Noah said.

"Why?" I asked, really wanting an answer.

"You were not in our circle of friends, you were brought in from the outside, into a group that already existed. I thought maybe someone didn't like it and was trying to get Ben to break-up with you," Noah began. "I also thought Ben pissed someone off and they were getting revenge, or someone in the lifestyle needed money."

"Anything else?" I asked.

"One more thing, the Detective also knew that we didn't want you to know any of it because Ben didn't want you upset before the wedding," Noah said. "Ben thought that you would do something stupid to protect us."

"I think he didn't want me to know because of Sophie," I said. "Well, the black mailer is getting his or her way. I just don't understand the GPS, were they trying to catch me cheating or something?"

"I really don't know," Noah confessed. There was another knock on the door. Noah opened it and Peggy whispered something and then left. "Ben is here wanting to see us."

"I'll stay here. I don't want to see him. I may beat the shit out of him if I do. Don't think you are getting away with anything either, I mad at you too," I said. I stood up and locked the main door and the bathroom door on his side. "This is the only door anyone can come in or out of. I don't want someone going after me when you're talking to Ben. Did Peggy and Beth know what was going on before all this happened here?" "Peggy, knew about the Ben stuff, but only a couple of people I trusted knew," Noah began. "Peggy told Beth after the stuff we found by that private detective and Beth told Peggy about the deliveries, when Peggy got the call about your office."

"Can you have Beth stay with me while you talk with Ben?" I asked.

"Yes, I can do that," Noah said going to the door and calling Beth. "Please stay with Avery."

"Yes sir," Beth said, and Noah left the room to see what else was going on. Beth came and sat on the couch with me. "You have a different ring on?"

"Can I ask you a question first about your lifestyle," I asked.

"Sure. What do you want to know?" Beth asked.

"Would you stay with someone if they had sex with a hard limit and they kept it from you?"

"I have left people for sleeping with my hard limits," Beth said. "If they do that you can't trust them. It will happen again, or that person will be in your life and make it a living hell, you end up being hurt worse in the long run."

"The ring is from Noah. We are getting married because Ben been sleeping with both of our hard limits," I said. "Ben thought I loved him enough that I would stay anyway."

"Sophie."

"Yep."

"You did the right thing. I had someone do it to me. I stayed, and it was the worst thing I couldn't done. I ended up leaving in the end," Beth said. We sat together not saying a word. I didn't like it being so quiet.

"Is there anything that I need to do or sign?" I asked.

"Yes, I'll get them for you," Beth said. I made my way over to my desk and sat down. Beth kept me busy for two hours before someone asked her to come talk to the police and the Detective. That is everything you need to do except read these files and tell them what you think?" she left the room, and Kim stepped in.

"It's after midnight, a new day and it doesn't look like it's getting any better," I said. "Is Ben still here?"

"Yes, he's in the conference room looking at the private detective stuff to see if there is anything he can think of," Kim began. "They went to pick up the Alan Anderson crew and Doug Dodson." "Why Doug?" I asked.

"It was his card that got the men in the building. The two men are not talking but they had a map to your office and Doug's card on them," Kim said. "They also picked up Sophie and there are three detectives here now and they are reviewing all the video's that Peggy's team found."

"Well, this day is getting better and better," I smirked. "Wish I could have seen that."

Chapter Eighteen

"Noah had them keep that fact from Ben because of today," Kim began. "Ben wants to see what happens to your old office, but they won't let him. Noah has security on Ben too."

"I bet Ben doesn't like that," I stated.

"He's also demanding to see you," Kim said.

My cell told me I had a text. I looked at it and it was Ben: I reread your texts from the other day, and you were telling Noah you were pregnant. Why didn't you tell me?

I texted back: I knew you would be mad you wanted to travel, and you wanted to wait. I wanted to tell you in person.

Not in a text.

Why did you tell Noah before me? Ben texted.

I was throwing up and my assistant thought I might be pregnant, and Noah wanted to take me home and I had my assistant get five tests and something to calm my stomach. I texted.

"Who are you texting?" Kim asked.

"Ben is asking questions, and I answering them. Can I ask you something?"

"Ask, if I can answer it I will," Kim said.

"If you had a hard limit and your main person slept with them, would you stay with them?" I asked.

"Sophie?" Kim questioned me and I nodded. "Everyone has to make that choice for themselves, but I had it happen to me, and I left him because trust is everything when you're in this lifestyle. I learned that the hard way at first and I never let it happen a second time."

"My first time I did this was in college, and he cheated with my best friend. I didn't have her as a hard limit, and I had some fun with them at first, but as I learned about hard limits there was a guy I couldn't stand, and I put him on the list. She brought him in to get me out and it worked. I swore I will never be in this lifestyle again. Then I met Ben and I'm back to the same place I was as before," I said.

"What does Noah want?" Kim asked.

"Me, even if I get out, Noah will stay with me, he is letting me decide. The thing is I know he likes men. I don't want to cut half of him off of who he is," I said. "Noah is hurting too right now, and having to be close to Ben is making him shut down and just work."

"That's not all the way true," Kim said. "Noah went off on
Ben in the conference room and is blaming all this on him."
"I think it has to do with both of them," I said.

"Why?" Kim asked.

"Because it affects Ben and Noah," I started. "Mr. Anderson is Noah's work and Sophie is connected with both of them. There has to be someone that is in Ben business that is connected to Sophie too."

"I think you're on to something," Kim started. "I need to text Peggy."

While she was texting Peggy, I got a text from Ben: I know Noah and you are mad at me right now, but I think we can make this work for all of us.

I texted back: You knew how Noah and I felt about Sophie. You still slept with her. I can never trust you not to do it again.

Ben texted back: This is all Noah's fault. It's his people.

I just put my cell down. "Now Ben is blaming all this on Noah."

"They think they have the two people from Ben's office, and they're looking for a connection with Sophie," Kim said.

"Peggy is coming to talk to you with one of the detectives."

There was a knock on the door, and Peggy and a man with a suit came in behind her. "Avery, this is Detective Warren."

"Hello, how can I help you?" I asked.

"They're pulling video from Ben's offices to see if Sophie is connected to the two people in Ben's office. At first it looked like to separate things, but you connected them. Can you tell me why you feel this way."

"First the private investigator had a file on all three of us and of Sophie too," I told him. "Alan Anderson wanted Noah two leave so he could be in charge again. Sophie told Anderson the only way to get Noah out is to get rid of me. His daughter was making my life hell She found out we were together and told everyone she was pregnant with Noah's baby to get Noah to pay her off. According to plans I would break up with Noah, leaving her father in charge again, and I would be fired." "How does Ben play in all this," Warren asked.

"Can I trust you not to let all this out to the news stations?" I asked.

"We keep important key parts out of the news, so what you tell me stays here," Warren stated.

"Ben and Noah will not sleep with people they work with," I informed him. "But Noah met me before I knew he was the head of this company. Ben and Noah were together with Sophie in college and during Christmas, I met Noah and Sophie. They were married at the time and Sophie was trying to get Ben to leave me for her and she didn't care that her husband was there when she was doing all this. They got a divorce in early February. Let's just say that Sophie and I do not like each other."

"When did Noah know you worked at his company?" Warren asked.

"We had a big office meeting about the company's owner that was coming in, that was about the middle of February. I was as shocked as he was that I worked for Noah, and he didn't know my last name so it didn't click that I worked for him. Ben knew I worked at Noah's company but never told either of us. He told us that he didn't think we would see each other again. Anyway, Noah moved in the first of March. We were doing very well of not letting anyone know we were together, until Noah told Cathy he couldn't be with her because he was in a relationship with me. To get her to stop chasing him. Cathy didn't take that well," I said. The detective was writing very fast.

"Are you dating both Ben and Noah?" Warren asked.

"We were all in a relationship together, and everything was going great until the middle of April when Ben started acting off to me. Working later, being out on business more. He told me she was trying to get all his business done before the wedding."

"When were you planning to get married," Warren asked.

"June first."

"The blackmailing started the first part of April," Warren said. "But I don't understand why you said the middle of April."

"That is when Ben started sleeping with Sophie," I stated.

"How do you know that?"

"I started getting more flowers, and Ben was overly protective of me. Plus, the paperwork we found in Anderson's safe shows when it started."

"When did you find out they were sleeping together?" Warren asked.

Chapter Nineteen

"Forty-eight hours ago," I said.

"That had to have been a shock but since you were with Noah why would you be upset about Sophie?" Warren asked. "I mean, you were in a open relationship with both men, what's the problem?"

"We have a open relationship, but we have to tell each other who we are sleeping with before we do it, so we all know. Ben hide all this from Noah and me," I said.

"I'm told your pregnant," Warren said, "When did you find this out?"

"Forty-eight hours ago. I'm twelve weeks along." "Do you know who the father is?" Warren asked.

"It has to be Ben or Noah," I said.

"Sophie says that she is three weeks along," Warren stated. "Who is the father?"

"Sophie says it's Ben's, and we have proof that she's been with at least four different men from the file we found in Anderson's office," I said. There was a knock on the door and a detective came in and whispered something to Warren and sat down next to him.

"This is a detective Tate," Warren said. "So, how did you know Sophie was sleeping with someone other than Ben at his office?"

"I've been in this room trying to understand how my life just went out of control. Ben kept the fact that he was being blackmailed, and no one told me until four hours ago that my plane crash was not an accident. Then Sophie yelled at Ben's place that 'I should have died in that plane crash, It got me thinking after I learned it wasn't a malfunction," I said.

"Did anyone else hear her say that?" Warren asked.

"Noah did, he was in the apartment too. We were waiting for Ben to come home."

"Tate, go ask him if Sophie said anything about the crash?" Warren said and Tate got up and left.

"Your right, Sophie was sleeping with one of the people so far and we are still looking," Warren said. "Would Sophie try to kill you to get Ben or Noah?"

"I don't know, but I do know she was trying to get me to break up with both of them," I said.

"That video you took of Sophie is very damaging. Why did you take it?" Warren asked.

"At Christmas, she said some hateful things to me, and Ben didn't believe me," I began. "Noah told me to set the video up because he didn't want her to know we had the files at the apartment. Noah took them to the car, and he knew she would try something. Like before, Ben wouldn't believe me. Ben has blinders on when it comes to Sophie."

Warren's cell went off, and he answered it. He didn't say anything to get any answer to what he was talking about. "At any time did you push Sophie when you were alone with her?"

"No, I set the video up before Noah left the apartment, to catch everything It's all on the video, and that was the only time I was alone with her," I said.

"Do you have the video with you," Warren asked. "We got one that looks like it was edited."

"I do, and Noah gave it to the security, and they called you. I didn't edit it," I said. I pulled out my cell and found the video and handed it to Warren to watch. When he was done, he did something and transferred my copy to his phone.

"Peggy, is this the one you saw and called me on?" Warren asked.

"Yes, what one did you get?" Peggy asked.

Warren took his cell and showed her the one he got. Peggy watched it and was pissed. "One of my people had to have edited that before it was sent."

Peggy grabbed her cell and asked, "I want Abbott to come to Noah's office."

"Sophie was rushed to the hospital because she thinks she is losing the baby and that it's your fault," Warren said. "I need Noah in here now."

Peggy started texting and Noah came in the room and sat down. "What can I help you with," Noah said.

"Both Ben and you are on my last nerve, and I don't want blame, I want answers. Got it?" Warren said.

I guess Ben and Noah are having trouble after all. "Ask your questions."

"Tell me what happened when Sophie came over," Warren asked.

Noah sat down next to me. "Sophie came over and told Avery to pack her bags because she was leaving. We had the files in the apartment, and I didn't want her to know I had them. We were eating dinner when Sophie showed up. She was being her usual self, mean to Avery even said Avery should have died in the plane crash. I told her to knock it off. I told Sophie and Avery I was taking them to the car. I told Avery to turn on her recorder because I didn't trust Sophie to be nice. I packed up the files and Avery went to the bedroom to pack her bags."

"Why were you packing your bags?" Warren asked me.

"I learned that Ben had lied to me about being with Sophie. He didn't come to my doctor's appointment after Sophie's, I just wanted to leave. I realized that Ben loved Sophie more than me," I said.

There was a knock on the door, and Abbott was there, "Have him wait," and someone closed the door. "What did you do next, Noah?"

"I told Sophie to stay on the couch until I got back. Then I took the files and ran down to my car. I moved quickly because I didn't want to leave Avery alone with Sophie. When I came back Sophie was in Ben and Avery's room and the video shows the rest," Noah said.

"Did you ever leave them alone after?" Warren asked.

"No, when Avery had her bags packed, I went to pack mine and Avery got her cell phone," Noah began. "Ben came home and there were words exchanged about Avery being pregnant and we went to the car, and I asked Avery if she recorded her. I saw Sophie hit Avery. I brought her here to report it. I texted Peggy a fast text to meet at my office. Peggy watched the tape and had you called and sent the tape to the department. When we were in my office, I found out Peggy was already here because of the break-in and had them report that to you, too."

"Can you three stay here while I question Abbott. Peggy, can you come with me?" Warren asked.

"I want answers because it looks like I'm firing someone this morning," Peggy said and they left the room, leaving Kim with us.

"Peggy is pissed," Kim said.

"What going on?" Noah asked.

"The video was edited before it was sent to the Police department. Sophie was rushed to the hospital because she stated that Avery pushed her and she is losing the baby now," Kim said.

"That sounds like Sophie but who edited the video?" Noah asked.

Chapter Twenty

"Peggy is trying to find out," I said. "Peggy saw the video you gave her and the edited one that was sent to the police. I guess it looks like I was hiding something the way it was edited."

"Did you see it?" Noah asked.

"No, only Peggy did," I said. "Warren wanted my copy, so he transferred it to his cell or to somewhere and gave me my cell back. The video is still on my cell."

"Ben said you're going back with him," Noah said. I knew Noah was on edge just like I was, I picked up my cell again and showed him the texts that he sent so he could read them.

"Thank you for letting me read it."

"Honestly, always," I said. "What's happening to have Warren ready to kill you both?"

"It started with Ben coming down saying the plane crash was my fault. Everything happened at once, and they had to pull Ben and me off of each other, but I got a good hit in," Noah said. "Sophie was picked up, and Ben started it again, blaming me for Sophie and that Sophie told him that I had been with her too."

"It started all over again," I said.

"Yep, so Ben has been confined to one of the offices and because he keeps starting stuff, Warren is ready to take him in," Noah said. "I know you came up with something because they wanted to know where you were and wouldn't let me come in. Ben keeps saying it's all my fault, and I think it's two separate things."

"No, it's all connected," Kim said. "Avery found the connection."

"So, how is it connected?" Noah asked. The door opened, and Peggy came in totally pissed off.

"Noah, Warren needs you in the other room," Peggy said. "Please charge him and fire his ass." Noah stood up and kissed me on the head and walked out of the room.

"Abbott edited the tape?" I asked.

"No, he gave it to a new guy to do it because he didn't want to do it," Peggy said. "Higgins did it because Sophie called him and asked him to. Plus, Abbott was sleeping with Sophie and was hiding it. When the police went through the files, someone deleted some of them, so they got a court order for the Hub for both companies. We only went after the missing files. We did most of the work for the police department, but the deleted files are of two of my people. I should have fired all of the kiss-asses that got along with that dumb ass I had to work, but I was giving everyone a second chance. Now I should have done what I wanted to do at the beginning. I talked to Noah about it and we agreed to have letters written for their files and give them a second chance." Peggy was pacing back and forth now, she was really pissed off. "I need to cool off and I don't see that happening any time soon."

"Peggy, Noah will need your help. I'll get you a punching bag for later but now you need to be there. Noah doesn't know everything," I said.

"You're right," Peggy said, taking a deep breath and walking out the door.

Chapter Twenty-One

It took two more hours before we were released to leave. When we were done, we went to this hotel Noah uses for business and guests to stay at. I was in the shower when Noah came in "Ben just texted, he went to the hospital and Sophie lost the baby. Then the police came and arrested her for attempted murder, stalking, blackmailing, and some other crimes."

I stuck my head out, "I just want to sleep and forget about all this," I said.

The next morning, we were all over the news, about how Ben had been cheating on me with Sophie, and she tried to kill me, not once, but three times. Sophie had also slept with two EEOs, one from Ben and Noah's company.

Later that morning, at work the police came back and explained how Sophie and Alan had tried to kill me with the earrings, apparently, they had poison on them. The third was when I was in the hospital, she paid for someone to kill me in the hospital and call it an accident. Sophie blackmailed him.

He came into the police station to report what she wanted him to do.

Peggy and three other people that Peggy trusted went through all the videos. Noah sent emails to everyone in the company and told them if they had any dealing with Sophie they should come forward. Only two came forward and talked to the police and they kept their jobs while others did not.

We found out that Doug was not involved in the crime, but he did let Cathy into his place, and she stole his card and gave it to her father. Noah had him transferred to a different state far from the Anderson family. Everyone involved was fired.

I had to call my parents and tell them that I was marrying Noah instead of Ben after everything that happened. My parents met him last month when they came down for the dress and tux fitting. My parents liked Noah more than Ben. Funny how parents see things you don't see in a relationship.

Noah and I are in a hotel looking for a new place to live. Noah's house was checked out from top to bottom. Peggy's group found cameras and listening devices all over the house. Noah doesn't trust that everything was found and put the house up for sale that day. Tiffany came down three days later and with Beth and Kim helping, we had everything transferred and changed to make the wedding still happen in ten days.

We sent cancel notices to all of Ben's business associates and other friends he invited. On my side we sent a change of groom notices out.

Tiffany told me I owed Ben a chance to explain just to have closer. Noah says I need to talk to him for some closer also Noah if he got closer from any of this?

Noah said he got it when they had to meet at the police station to fill in the blanks about some of the things that happened.

Three days before the wedding I met Ben outside the coffee shop, it was the first time I had seen him since the night everything had blown up around me. I ordered a lemonade and sat and listened to him. I started to remember the first time we met and all the time together and came up with something I had never seen before, I was so stupid. I thought. When Ben was done, he asked if I could forgive him. "You only saw me as your temporary girlfriend and treated me that way." I left the coffee shop for the last time. I had my closer.

Chapter Twenty-Two

The day before the wedding Noah, Jeremy, Alex, and I slowly rose the following day. Alex and Jeremy were here to take pictures for the wedding and honeymoon fun. I had a few last-minute things to attend to, and there was a rehearsal and dinner that night. We had rented a apartment until we could find a house we wanted. The wedding ceremony was to be Saturday afternoon at four o'clock, so I'd even have some time Saturday morning to do some errands too.

Noah and I made love in the morning. After breakfast, Alex and I packed overnight bags. We were going to stay in Noah's hotel not far from Emerald Chapel in Seattle where the wedding would take place. Alex and I were going to share a room together.

We left Noah and Jeremy to their own devices for the day, and we took Noah's Porsche and headed north out of the City. Noah had arranged for a car service for him later on that day. He said he was going out to the airport to pick up a large portion of the wedding party, some were going to our Caribbean Island for the honeymoon. We were firm believers in 'group' honeymoons.

As we drove, I called and reached Tiffany on her cell phone. A very pregnant Melissa and Jennifer, Ben's sisters, had arrived the night before and were staying at the same hotel. They squealed with delight to know we'd see them in a few minutes.

I'd met Tiffany the year before when she'd married Mark, however the two had lived together for two years already and included Melissa in their family. Now Melissa was pregnant with 'their' child, and they were both ecstatic. Jennifer and hubby Brad were there too, along with their dear friends Beth and Doug. All of us shared an intimate relationship with one another more than once over the past year.

I called my Mom next. My Mom and Dad, along with my older sister Amy, were on their way and would be here in late afternoon to connect with all of us and participate in the wedding rehearsal that night. They had a room at the same hotel too. I also got an update about which of my relatives intended to show up for the wedding and reception.

Alex and I checked in at the hotel and amidst a hail of kisses and hugs as we joined up with Tiffany, Melissa and Jennifer. We fawned over Melissa who expected to deliver her baby within the month. We took turns feeling her extended belly as the baby turned and kicked. I wasn't feeling Peanut, and I was just starting to show. I told my parents I was pregnant to give them time to accept it, but Mom was so excited about being a grandma it didn't seem to matter.

With the exception of Melissa who drove, the rest of us walked downtown from the hotel and had lunch. We then walked back, but not before visiting every clothing and knick-knack shop on the way.

The rehearsal at Emerald Chapel took a short time thanks to a well-prepared minister whom Tiffany had well briefed with an outline of the service. Soon a crowd of twenty of us gathered in the restaurant for cocktails, hors d'oeuvres, and then dinner. Toasts were made and Noah and I had fun handing out joke gifts and remembrances to our close friends and family members.

After dinner, people left for their rooms and homes. Tiffany, Melissa and Mark whispered to me that they could barely wait for the 'honeymoon' and playing together. When Brad and Jennifer kissed me goodnight, they said they really wished we could be together, but they too, would wait for our island adventure. Beth and Doug made similar comments.

In short order Alex and I found ourselves alone in our room. As I shut the door behind us I turned and raised an eyebrow to the coy look she gave me over her shoulder.

"Just because everyone else flaked out on you doesn't mean that I will," she said with a licentious grin.

"I promised Noah no sex with anyone else tonight," I replied.

"How about a good movie then?" Alex asked.

"Sounds good," I said. I remain convinced that women are much better lovers than men. Not that Noah isn't attentive, inventive and sensitive; it's just that he has to search to find the right spots. Alex knew instinctively where to kiss, where to lick, where to suck, where to blow, and where to bite.

My cell phone went off, and Noah's face showed on my cell.

"Hi honey."

"Remember when I said no sex tonight..." Noah began.

"Who is it with?" I asked.

"Jeremy and Brad," Noah said.

"As long as I can be with Alex, you have a deal," I said. Alex School perked right up hearing that.

"Have fun, love," Noah said.

"You too," I hung up.

Chapter Twenty-Three

My parachute was slow to bring me down to earth. During my bliss, I thought of all the people I loved and the ways love materialized. I felt everyone's love and was prescient about how it sustained my own bliss and joy.

Somewhere I think I dozed off but only for a few seconds.

My body needed to retreat from the high state of stimulation Alex had created. We kissed for a long time, and I told her how I loved Noah, Jeremy, and her.

I slid down Alex's pliant body until I could suckle on one of her breasts. I brought the teat into my mouth and rapidly agitated the nipple. I felt Alex stiffen as I did this erotic act. Soon I was on her pussy, her clitoris, and her entire lower body.

Soon I was the aggressor, my fingers and then hand invading her nether region and bringing her to orgasm after orgasm. Alex moaned, squirmed, writhed, and groaned under my attention.

Alex went to that orgasmic state I'd just left. I kept her there, almost torturing her body with my love for her.

Then I was the one whose head was grabbed and pushed solidly against her pussy; my nose buried in her vagina... inhaling the sweet aroma as I licked the only space I could reach.

Then stillness.

Then kisses and love.

Then slumber, our naked bodies entwined around one another.

In the morning, I awoke to find Alex staring at me in a most loving way. We kissed again for a little while, cooing at each other about the day and how much fun we'd have leading up to my wedding.

We showered and dressed casually, then went downstairs to find several of the others already at breakfast. We joined them.

By ten o'clock I'd rounded up all my attendants, and we headed downtown to a spa. I followed Tiffany's lead about getting everyone super pampered for the afternoon wedding. I, however, had made some special arrangements.

The group included Tiffany, Melissa, Jennifer, Beth, Alex, and Amy, my sister who for the last year or so had lived in Paris working for Google Europe. I thought Amy was a liberal thinker and shared most of the same values I did. However, I wasn't sure about how much to tell her about my polyamorous relationships or my bisexuality.

The first hour in the spa consisted of a pedicure, manicure, and some group time nude in the sauna. Everyone behaved, although I worried about Tiffany, but not for what you would think. Ben kept coming into my head even now. I know we did the right thing but it didn't stop me from thinking of what if.

Then my special surprise started. The spa directed the seven of us into a large room with massage tables arranged in a large circle with the head of each table facing inward. At each table stood a very attractive and muscular masseuse in a white tshirt, white shorts and white tennis shoes, ready to attend to each one of us. This was better than I'd expected for each guy was over six feet tall and a true Adonis in looks and physique.

I sensed a little hesitation as the women entered the room clad only in their towels, chose a table, and lay face down while clutching the towel to their bodies. I could hear a series of introductions being made by each masseuse; my masseuse said his name was Will.

Each man rubbed some warmed oil into the shoulders and back of each of us. Their touch was tender, and the aroma of the oil was alluring. I looked around and each man seemed to know what he was doing. They worked up and down our legs briefly telling us they'd return there for a deeper massage in a moment. I really started to relax although I knew the gist of what was going to happen next.

One by one each of the men told the woman they were working on that they were too warm and so they were going to shed some of their clothing. Will, for instance, then pulled his t-shirt over his head and kicked off his white shoes. Next, he jerked down his shorts until all he was wearing was a male thong clearly filled with a generous inflated cock. He had my attention.

I looked around the room at the other six men as they restarted their massages. Several of the men were more excited than the others and their cocks were barely contained in their small cloth sacks.

Will lifted the towel from my body and I saw all the towels disappear as the men worked oil into the areas of our back and buttocks that they hadn't touched before.

Our eyes roamed the gorgeous landscape taking in the muscular men as they attended to us and rubbed us into not only a relaxed state but also a state of sexual excitement. Occasionally our eyes met one of the other women and we winked or looked agog at what was happening.

At one point Will stood by my head and rubbed his hands deeply down my back and shoulders. His barely clothed cock frequently brushed along parts of my face as he worked on me.

I resisted the urge to grab and suck.

"Do you want me to do your front as well?" Will asked me in a smooth, subdued voice.

I told him, "I wouldn't miss this for the world." We grinned at each other, and I rolled over, completely exposing myself to him.

I noted that we led the way for soon I heard the other women getting on their backs. Oddly enough, we girls weren't talking to each other very much.

Now the moans started as our bodies were oiled again and with muscular hands the warm oil rubbed into our entire bodies, including breasts, abdomens, and then down our legs. After twenty minutes, we were turned on our fronts again.

The men gave us deep back rubs to end the session and then one by one escorted us to the showers. Will led the way. He carefully placed a cap on my hair telling me the hairdo was next on the agenda. Under the spray in the large communal shower, he washed me from head to foot, using a loofah and small brush here and there on my body. I never felt so clean in all my life.

The others joined us as they finished their adjacent massage room, each man attending to the woman he'd massaged. I watched as Melissa's attendant paid particularly loving care to her full body; it seemed so tender to see the obvious affection he had for her and in her condition.

A skin lotion got applied to us as well and strong hands rubbed the lotion into our bodies. My skin just tingled. I don't know that I'd ever felt so pampered. We were provided with a large terry cloth robe and directed into the hair salon part of the spa. The men disappeared.

Our hair treatments took an hour and proved to be as relaxing as the past hour with the men. Now we started talking again amongst ourselves and then with the stylists. Most of the stylists had peeked in while we had our 'massages' and were amazed at the quality of the men I'd arranged to 'service' us for our massages.

By one-thirty, we were not only sexually sated for the moment but also dolled up, made-up, well fed, and looking like million dollars. Most of us drove back to the Hotel. I finally got my sister alone for a few minutes when Alex, Beth, Jennifer, Tiffany and Melissa went off to find their husbands.

I hadn't spent much time with my older sister since she left home to go to college years earlier. We kept in touch with occasional phone calls or e-mails and I perhaps saw her once or twice a year at my parent's home when she came to visit. However, many siblings have been missing closeness in our relationship since she moved away.

As we walked into the hotel, I said to her, "Did you like the massage?"

"Loved it," She paused then said, "I'm not the prude you probably think I am, in fact I'm pretty free thinking about sex and relationships. You must be too, based on what you set up for us today. From seeing your friends, I'd thrown in with a pretty free-thinking bunch too."

I smiled at her and said, "Yes, we've all been together in one way or another before today. I've always thought that love and physical attraction were in short supply."

Amy pulled me into the bar area and we ordered two glasses of wine. She said, "I don't want you to talk to Mom or Dad about this, okay?" I nodded in agreement. "I was a swinger for several years, although things have come to a stand still since I moved to Paris. I've never met anyone I really cared for over there. To tell the truth I miss the love, excitement and support I felt from my intimate friends I had in California."

Slowly, I told her, "Noah and I have shared ourselves with others too." I could see her relaxing in my sharing. I'd suddenly become another like-minded soul and a co-conspirator. I told her, "The 'group honeymoon' will be full of 'sharing' too."

Amy asked carefully, "And you're okay with all that?"

"Oh, I'm more than okay with it but Ben decided to be with someone I said no to. I was with Ben and Noah; that's how I met Noah. We loved Ben but he didn't love us back the same way. I discovered that I'm bisexual. In fact, our honeymoon will be the first time we've all been together in a while... in a permissive environment."

Amy leaned across the small bar table and kissed me on the cheek. "I discovered I'm bisexual as well. I took such delight in that discovery with my friends out west. At first, I limited myself to men, but in our lovemaking, we often got very close to each other. Well, I tried to understand what turned on the men so much and I ended up turned on too," Amy stated.

"I started in college with Alex. I should introduce you two more intimately. She and Jeremy, who you met last night, live in London. If the chemistry works you might at least have someone on that side of the Atlantic you could be close to," I said laying it all out.

"I'll go out of my way to get to know them better tonight at the reception," Amy said.

I thought for a moment and blurted out, "Amy, why don't you come down to the Caribbean with us. Come on the honeymoon. Oh, please. We're all billing it as a big party anyway and Alex and Jeremy will be there. I don't think anyone would think anything other than that you're just one more reveler."

Amy studied me for a long time. I wasn't sure if she was weighing the sincerity of my invitation or thinking about whether she could spare the time off work or what.

Then she said slowly, "I'd like that very much. You're sure I won't be a fifth wheel or anything?"

"Not a bit, in fact you'll even out the ratio if I count correctly. The house we rented has plenty of space." I grinned.

Amy said, "This whole conversation, that's all I've been thinking about. Do you think I'm crazy? I'd like to make love with Tiffany and Noah too. I've had the hots for him since I met him that day last summer when you brought him up too Mom and Dad's home for dinner while I was visiting.

"He briefly mentioned that he thought you were pretty 'hot' too, as I recall," I told her. Amy laughed and nodded.

We continued to open up to each other about our sex lives and how we felt about open relationships and various sexual situations. I shared with Amy some of the intimate times I'd had with Mark, Tiffany and Melissa and with Jennifer, Brad, Beth and Doug. I also told her about the intimate relationships with my flight instructors Greg and David, since both of them were in the wedding and, I hoped, down on the Island for the honeymoon party.

"Now jealousy is finding out that you joined the Mile High Club with two hunks while your ex-fiancé flew the plane." Amy said to me with a smirk, "Oh, dear me! I just realized I don't have a thing to wear down on the Island and ... and how are we getting there? Do I need to phone for airline tickets?"

"No, no. You don't have to worry about anything except delaying your trip back to Paris from Seattle by a week or so. You can have one of my bikinis, although if the past is prolog, you'll need a thong to wear most of the time. As for getting there, Noah arranged to borrow another corporate jet for the week. Greg and I will pilot the plane down on Monday morning with everyone aboard. You'll have time to see Mom and Dad some more tomorrow and poke through my wardrobe, although you won't need many clothes." As an afterthought, I tossed in, "We just fuck all the time!"

"Oh, I am so going to join you," Amy said with a twinkle in her eye. "I hope your last remark is an understatement." We grinned lecherously at each other as I nodded in the affirmative.

Alex walked into the hotel about that time, saw us in the bar and joined us. She had a rosy look to her complexion from her brisk walk.

"Amy's just decided to join us on the Island," I told her as she sat down next to us.

Alex's eyebrows went up with an unasked questions.

Chapter Twenty-Four

"Oh, yes," I said to Alex. "Didn't you notice this morning? Amy was in there with her masseuse like the rest of us."

"The only thing I noticed for an hour this morning was a ten-inch cock that had my name on it. That was the nicest bridesmaid gift I've ever gotten...a fabulous fuck!" Alex turned to Amy and asked, "I take it you availed yourself of the gift as well?"

"Of course. The group setting made it that much more erotic and exciting. I love to fuck. Besides, I think I have exhibitionist and voyeur genes in my system," Amy grinned and spoke.

Alex turned to me, "She'll fit in well on the Island. Bring her for sure." We all laughed, then Alex rose, came beside Amy, leaned in and kissed her...a long, sensuous kiss that I could tell elevated the temperatures of both women.

Just as Alex broke off the kiss and sat down again, my parents walked in the door of the hotel. Their presence shut down any further conversation about our sex lives. I thought it strange that their two daughters had these lascivious feelings about life and love, we couldn't share them with the people they should be closest to. I guess this is what generation gaps are all about.

Mom told me it was time to think about dressing and getting serious about the rest of the wedding preparations. I'd explained time and again that Tiffany was handling the entire thing. I think my Mom was actually put out that she had to do so little to help me prepare for my wedding; my ex-future sister-in-law had done almost all of it.

We walked upstairs to our rooms. Mom joined Alex as the two of them started to prep me for my gown. I think I shocked my mother by stripping and walking around the room in nothing but a frilly and lacy blue thong I'd borrowed from Alex. Alex cheered me on wearing 'something borrowed' and 'something blue' at the same time.

Jeremy knocked on the door as I pranced around poking at the dress, veil and all the undergarments. He said through the door, "I'm here to take pictures, and candids for the wedding album."

Alex looked at me. Knowing it was a bit of a white lie for my mother's benefit, I said, "Well, let him in. He's seen you naked before; we're built about the same. No surprise there." My mother rolled her eyes towards heaven.

Jeremy politely said hello to my mother, set his camera bag down, and pulled out his Canon. He said to me without blinking an eye at my near nudity, "You just do what you do naturally. I may ask you to pause or turn, but other than that, these are all candid shots."

I nodded and returned to pulling the dress out of its protective bag and fluffing up the crinolines. I kept hearing the shutter snap. I even watched as he caught one of my Mom and Alex working on the veil and short train.

Mom whispered to me at one point, "Shouldn't you at least put on a brassiere? I mean, there's a man in the room."

I told her, "Oh, Mom. He's going to see me topless on the beach in two days. Who knows, maybe I'll even go nude. Don't worry about it. His wife is here, after all." I could see Alex and Jeremy both stifling laughs over her shoulder. Mom rolled her eyes some more and then announced that she was going back to her room to slip into her special dress and would be right back. She left the room.

After the door had closed, Jeremy and Alex burst out laughing, and I joined them. "You sure don't make it comfortable for the older set, do you?" Alex chided. I grinned.

"Hold up the veil in front of you," Jeremy said. I like this light from the window...stand over there. Just like that. I can see your breasts through the thin fabric, a very erotic shot. The camera clicked about ten times as I turned back and forth and posed for him.

He directed again, "Alex step in and hold her from the back. Like that, more your arm around her." Click. Click. Click. "Now cup her breast in your hand. Good." Click. Click. Click.

"All right," he said, "Enough erotica for now. Go back to what you were doing, although I know I'm going to hate seeing you cover up such a lovely body."

I walked to him and kissed him. "Thank you for so many things. You are such goodness in my life ... and in Alex's life. Thank you." I kissed him again. He gently rubbed one nipple with a thumb.

I stayed undressed and helped Alex slide into her dusty rose-colored bridesmaid dress. She looked so pretty in the dress and the folds of the dress did amazing things for her breasts and backend. Jeremy offered that he'd be ready for a 'quickie' anytime she was willing. I think he actually got a picture of her nearly naked body as I copped a feel before sliding the dress over her head.

When my mother returned, I was pretty well into the wedding gown. I thought that brides probably spend more time looking at and talking about getting into a gown than the few seconds it actually takes to put it on and adjust it to their bodies.

I'd worn the white shoes around the condo on and off over the past month so I'd broken them into the point they were comfortable to wear for long time periods. With all the dancing and standing I planned, I didn't want to be disadvantaged with a pair of shoes that hobbled me before the day was out.

Mom buzzed around, twitching at my dress. Amy, Tiffany, Melissa, Beth and Jennifer came in resplendent in their bridesmaid's gowns. The gowns were floor length, high waist pastel sheaths with a revealing bodice. I noticed it would be even more revealing when they bent forward. Of course, we'd all planned it that way.

Melissa made a show in her lavender dress. The combination of the high waist and the fact the other dresses were sheaths made it all the more evident that she was very pregnant. She exaggerated by pulling the dress tight against her thighs, which amplified the evidence of her impending child. Melissa said, "If I do this, every OB/GYN within twenty miles will drop everything and run to my aid." She thought for a moment as she looked at herself in a floor length mirror and added, "I also look like a purple Easter egg."

We laughed and I went and hugged her. "Melissa, I love you so. Thank you for doing this. I know you feel conspicuous but if we'd waited a month, we'd had a screaming baby in the back of the chapel." I poked at the baby then felt her stomach; the baby poked back.

"Smart kid you have there. Got a name yet?"

"We do," Melissa said softly. She turned to Tiffany. "Should we tell her?"

Tiffany teared up and said, "Yes. It's time to tell her."

Melissa hugged me again and said, "We're going to call the baby 'Avery'... after you. We love you so much and you've brought such happiness to our lives... and Noah. The middle name is going to be 'Grace' after Jennifer and Tiffany's mother, plus she'll have a choice of first names all the way through her life."

"I teared up. "Thank you. You didn't have to do that. I'm so honored that you think of me this way." I hugged and kissed Melissa on the lips then did the same to Tiffany. My mother looked on in pleased amazement over what was taking place and how we interacted. In the distance I heard the persistent click of the camera.

"How will we know when to go over to the Emerald Chapel?" my mother finally asked, trying to refocus our attention on the last of the dressing details and the wedding.

Tiffany responded, "Mark will call my cell phone with a fiveminute warning. If you look out your window you can still see a lot of people arriving at the church. They have to walk by here to get to it...oh, there goes Uncle Ted and Aunt Mel." I peeked out the window over her shoulder.

Tiffany went on, "When we get the signal, we'll all troop over and the ushers will be ready for us in the foyer off the Chapel." She turned to my mother and said, "You'll be seated then the processional will begin. Did I tell you there's a jazz group in addition to the organ?"

"NO," I said surprised. "That's wonderful." I hugged Tiffany again. Again, with a tear in my eye I thanked her for all her hard work. Tiffany explained how she'd adjusted the service to get some modern music into the wedding service.

We sat and chatted as we waited for the phone call. Jeremy hung in there with us taking photos for a while then slipped away. "Time to get the groom's side of things," he'd told us.

Chapter Twenty-Five

Ten minutes later the phone rang. Mark told Tiffany to wait another five minutes then come over. We waited then slowly walked downstairs.

The Emerald Chapel is a huge, red brick church with a slate roof that telegraphs establishment and strong New England roots. It has a steeple that is clearly a direct line with God. The setting, with large trees around it, is right out of a storybook. Our little entourage walked slowly from the hotel to the Chapel, a distance of only a hundred yards. Alex walked behind me holding my short train and skirt off the ground as I held the front of my gown up a foot or so. We ascended the dozen or so stairs to the front entrance of the building.

Mark, Brad, Doug, Greg and David were all there as ushers for the wedding as well as groomsmen. Jeremy snapped photos from a corner of the vestibule. Mark and Brad escorted my mother down the aisle. I know she loved arriving with a handsome young man on each arm, plus she did look very fetching in her wedding dress. Even for a middle-aged woman she'd retained her youthful shape. We all peeked into the huge door, as it swung open. The sanctuary was full of people on both sides of the church. We let the door swing shut.

"Daddy are you ready to go?" I asked as I hugged my Dad's arm to me.

"Yes. I want to tell you I am so proud of you, Avery," my Dad said. "You and Amy have been a delight to me every day of my life since your arrival on this planet. Noah and friends are all such wonderful people; I love them all. Some make me wish I was thirty years younger too!" He gave me a kiss and reached over and squeezed Amy's hand. I loved my Dad.

Brad and Mark arrived back at the huge doors to the sanctuary and propped them open. We stood out of sight off to one side. They had laid out a snow-white runner for me to walk on down the entire aisle of the church. Further, they'd draped both sides of the aisle with a running garland of greenery with white flowers woven into it. At each pew, a bouquet graced the aisle.

Tiffany came up, "Oh, I almost forgot your bouquet." She thrust into my hand a large and beautiful gathering of spring flowers. A small handle had been created for me to clasp as I held the flowers. She passed out smaller bouquets to the other women.

The groomsmen slipped down a side aisle to join the groom at the front of the church. Jeremy took a few more shots then left to get down front to photograph the entrance processional and the main part of the wedding.

We all heard the organ crank up with the wedding processional cue. My sister led the procession to the front of the church followed by Tiffany and Melissa walking side by side; Melissa's 'bump' prominence not hard to miss. Jennifer and Beth followed together at the appropriate interval followed by Beth. As they arrived at the front of the church, each bridesmaid set her flowers on a small table in front of the first pew.

The minister and my friends formed a circle on the large, raised platform at the front of the sanctuary. Each woman joined her partner as she arrived at the stage, so the circle was not the traditional men on one side and women on the other. Noah stood alone in the midst of the circle as the others held hands in a circle around him.

My Dad escorted me down the aisle. As we passed the first pew, I set my flowers on the small table. At the circle, Amy and Greg dropped their hands to admit me into the circle. Just before I left his arm, Dad gave me a kiss, and I walked into the circle to face Noah. My Dad walked back to the first pew and my mother stood and joined him; they walked up to the circle and joined hands between Amy and Greg. The people that loved us most surrounded Noah and me.

The minister began, "Thank you all for joining this couple as they openly pledge their love to each other today. This union represents a desire by Noah Hopkins and Avery Hart to share and explore life more fully with each other, to add strength and support to one another, and, through each other, to amplify the joy the universe provides us all and the love they feel for each other and for life."

At that point, Tiffany broke from the circle and came to the front of the group on stage. She recited a poem perfectly. It was *Elizabeth Barrett Browning's 'Sonnet Number 43' - 'How Do I Love Thee,'*. I got all choked up as she finished.

As Tiffany joined the circle, the minister continued. "Noah and Avery are adults and give themselves to the other freely.

They cherish this union and all it represents. They encourage each other's journeys through life, being not a tether but added strength in those travels; being not a yoke but a constant companion, whether present or not; being committed to the other without ownership; caring without possessing; and striving to help each other be complete individuals."

Jennifer now broke from the circle and came forward to face the congregation. Like her sister, she flawlessly recited *Susan Polis Shultz's* poem, *'Just In Case You Need To Know...'* As she read, as she finished and turned, Jennifer gave me a wink and then kissed Brad as she rejoined the circle. It was telling how

Ben's sisters supported me and Ben couldn't. I wonder if Noah is thinking the same thing.

The minister picked up the thread of the service again; "The bonding agent for this union is love. All of us here today share that love for this couple and for each other. Please join hands so that the love can flow through us all." The entire church rustled as people held hands. I could see people reaching across the pews so that even the pews were connected together.

The reverend said strongly, "The love Noah and Avery share will not court jealousy, for where there is jealousy, there is no love. This love will encompass others, for where there is love it expands to be inclusive. This love has many levels, for love is physical and spiritual, personal and familial, an honor and a joy. Love is why we're here."

At this point Melissa broke from the circle and waddled to the front. She had a silly grin at the humor of her appearance.

She recited *'E. E. Cummings'* poem *'I Carry Your Heart With Me.'*

Behind me the jazz combo started to play. A beautiful young chocolate-colored long black-headed woman in a shimmery forest green cocktail dress came forward from the corner where she'd been sitting. I knew from Tiffany that her name was Tymea Shane and that she'd done some jazz recordings. She did a beautiful rendition of the well-known song by Amy Grant, 'That's What Love is For.' She was so professional in handling the song, and her voice was so pure that by the end there wasn't a dry eye in the house. Led by our whole circle, the whole congregation applauded enthusiastically. The song certainly underscored all the reasons to love someone. Noah had this added to the ceremony. Noah wanted something of him in it and I agreed to all of it being changed but he had helped us with he poems and I think this was something he really wanted.

Alex came forward at that point, facing the hundreds in the pews and recited an *Roy Croft* poem that started with the line, *'I love you not only for what you are, but for what I am when I am with you. I love you not only for what you have made of yourself but for what you are making of me. I love you for the part of me that bring out...* ' I couldn't help stifling a sob as she spoke of my love for Noah. I looked at Noah "*I love you.*" Noah mouthed and he had a tear running down his cheek. I added a couple of things and took out something Ben had wanted.

Beth replaced Alex at center stage and read a poem by *Noah* with the last line '*When I met you I had no idea where our relationship would lead us; how beautiful you would make my world. But now I know without a doubt the luckiest day of my life was the day that I met you.*' Beth turned and blew me a kiss as she returned to her place in the circle.

The minister refocused everyone on the circle by asking, "Noah, please state your vows to Avery, and Avery your vows to Noah." The circle parted so that everyone in the congregation could watch the two of us.

Noah held both my hands in his. I got all teary as I looked in his beautiful eyes. He began speaking with a strong clear voice, "Avery, I, Noah, will be your partner forever. I will cherish you and this union, and hold your joy above my own. I will love you more each new day and always treat you with the utmost care and respect. There is no circumstance that you will face in which you will not find my full support and my love. There will be nothing that I do not share with you. I pledge you my love."

I had a tear running down my face as he squeezed my hands in his. He looked at me with such love. I began to speak, trying to remember to speak up so everyone could hear me, "Noah, I, Avery, pledge you my love and life forever. I will cherish you and our marriage, be devoted to you, be supportive of you, be respectful of you, be caring of you, be sharing with you, and be loving with you always. Your joy will be my joy, your burden mine to help carry, your dreams mine to help make happen, your life my happiness to embrace."

After a short silence, the minister said, "These vows of love stand before us all on this happy and joyous day for Avery and Noah."

The jazz combo started another song and Tymea Shane stood again. She smiled at us then sang a jazzy version of *'Our Love Is Here to Stay.'* Again, she got a large round of applause from everyone. I wondered how Tiffany found such great tAllent and then got them to appear at my wedding.

The minister started again as soon as the song ended; "Having witnessed these vows and by the power vested in me by the state of Washington, I am happy to now pronounce Noah and Avery as man and wife." He held his arms in the air in the form of a blessing from the universe over the two of us.

I moved into Noah's arms as he embraced me and he kissed me. I fought to hold back my tears of happiness. After our perfunctory kiss I hugged him and he held me. For that brief second, the whole world disappeared, and I felt the infinite depth of our love.

We turned and the circle of our dear friends swarmed in and surrounded us for a minute with hugs and kisses. Then the circle parted and allowed us forward. Everyone stood and applauded about that time. The jazz combo started again and as we led the exit procession, Tymea sang *'Groovy Kind of Love'* — a dreamy love song that had many people swaying in time to the music.

Noah and I reached the back of the chapel and I suddenly realized that Ben was sitting in the back row. I had no idea what to do next. Noah was also at a loss of words when he saw him. Tiffany appeared a few seconds later moving us to where we needed to be next not seeing her brother there at all. She herded us all into a receiving line and as the first couple came from the sanctuary, she routed them into the line. That started the line so that eventually we were congratulated and met everyone that had been at the service.

After a round of photos with all sorts of combinations of people and relatives, we filed into a large limousine and were whisked about two miles away for our reception. As we got into the limousine it was the first time we both could talk. "Did you see who I saw?" Noah asked me.

"Yes, why did he show up?" I wandered.

"Wanted to see if we go through with it."

"Do you think he has regrets now?"

"I think he does now but not before," Noah began. "Sophie has a way of making you feel like you're doing the right thing even though everyone else will tell you differently."

"I don't want to think about it," I said as we stopped and the door was opening up. Ben had put both of us in a sad state and I didn't want to feel that way. Not today. More photos were taken there followed by all the pre-dinner silliness that goes on. Dinner started with round after round of toasts and glass tapping so Noah and I would kiss.

After dinner we cut the cake and sedately did not mash the cake into each other's faces. We did kiss a lot, however. We did the traditional dances with each other, with Dad and Mom, with relatives, and then with everybody. The band was rocking' and the crowd hung in there and enjoyed the great music right up to the end. I was glad too that the jazz quartet and Tymea Shane reappeared for a half-hour gig while the rock band took a break.

Things broke up at midnight when the band finally stopped.

Ben's sisters, their husbands and the others headed back to the hotel. We informed my Mom and Dad that Amy was coming with us to the Island. My parents actually thought that was a wonderful idea and were glad we'd get some time together. I told Mom and Dad that we would visit before we left on Monday.

Chapter Twenty-Six

I'm married. Wow!

I'm Mrs. Avery Hopkins.

Do I like that name? I could keep my maiden name – Hart; I could remain Avery Hart. Noah could become Noah Hart instead of Noah Hopkins. I could do a hyphen: Mrs. Avery Hart-Hopkins or Mrs. Avery Hopkins-Hart. We could both do a hyphen. Decisions. Decisions. I'd have to talk to Noah when he and the other men returned from their golf game. I thought it amazing that we hadn't thought about this at all.

As I pondered my name and other deep questions, I floated in the pool at the L'Oasis, a private villa we'd arranged for our honeymoon party on several acres of land on St. Maarten. The estate consisted of a large Moroccan-style home with seven master bedrooms, several other bedrooms, two pools – an Olympic size 'negative edge' pool by the house and a smaller pool down by the beach, an eight person Jacuzzi (that we had fourteen people in the night before), and a vista of the waters where the Caribbean Sea kisses the Atlantic Ocean.

The view from the patio around the pool was spectacular. One perspective looked across the water to some of the hills making up the rest of St. Maarten; the other view looked across the Caribbean Sea where dozens of small yachts and ketches played against the azure sea. Further, the temperature was a balmy eighty-five degrees.

There were fourteen of us partying at L'Oasis – all on our honeymoon: Noah and I, the newlyweds as of three days earlier; Mark, Melissa and Tiffany – the ménage a trois surrounding Tiffany, one of Ben's sisters; Brad and Jennifer – Ben's other sister; Doug and Beth – intimate friends of Brad and Jennifer and now all of us; my sister Amy; and two men that had been Ben and my flight instructors for the Cessna Citation jet – Greg and Mike.

Greg and I had flown Brad, Jennifer, Doug, Beth, Mike, and Amy down in a rented Cessna Citation. We rented a plane because Noah doesn't own a plane but plans to buy one now. This trip was the first I'd flown since the crash. I was reluctant to pilot the Citation down to the Island but Noah insisted so that I would get my 'sea legs' back after the accident. By the time I landed I had regained some of my excitement about aviation.

Noah and I hadn't participated, however, all our passengers availed themselves of the opportunity to join the Mile High Club during our flight to St. Maarten's from Seattle – with a refueling stopover in Jacksonville mandated by headwinds on the trip down. Once during the flight, a very odiferous and nude Amy came into the cockpit and kissed the two of us. She tried to persuade Greg to come back and make love to her but he begged off in favor of a more relaxed time in the evening.

Greg and Mike were going back to grab more people that had flown the rest from the Wichita Flight Safety Center where they worked and were part owners. As in the other plane, the passengers – and pilots taking turns in this case – played in the Mile High Club on their way to the Island. Tiffany, of course, insisted on having her picture taken sitting naked on Greg's lap and impaled on his long cock as they flown along at 40,000-feet. Alex took the pornographic picture but only if Tiffany took a similar photo of her. There were other photos too that Jeremy later shared with us from his laptop.

We'd landed in mid-afternoon on Monday and it was almost five o'clock by the time our large party got to L'Oasis. We were all nude in the pool within five minutes of our arrival.

Everyone understood the Island's dress code.

We found the Villa well stocked for our arrival and soon everyone had a beer or wine and hors d'oeuvres to nibble on as they basked in the sun or floated in the upper pool. We were a frisky bunch, and there was no end to erotic play and suggestions about how we could all spend our night. A few of us ran down the steps to the beach and splashed in the Caribbean just to feel the soft salt water on our bodies.

The first night at the Villa Noah and I made love to one another, taking turns being the one being pleasured by the other one. Even with the events of the past few days and our love making the previous night I remained incredulous yet ecstatic about my relationship with him.

Amy and I woke early and went for a run down the beach. Both of us conceded the use of sports bras to control the sway and oscillation of our breasts as we ran. We shed our bras and running shorts as soon as we returned to the Villa. We were sitting nude in the kitchen talking as some of the others started to arrive in a similar state of dress.

The kitchen in the Villa opened into a huge family room and into a media center in another direction. A formal dining room that could seat us all opened into a Great Room, complete with a cathedral ceiling and a balcony running around the upstairs perimeter off of which the large bedrooms flowed. Even for its size, the house design favored close and intimate relationships. Outside the bedrooms, a shared porch ran the length of the house and looked out over the Caribbean.

Amy and I welcomed people into the kitchen by walking up to the individual and pressing our bodies into them as we gave them a sincere and loving kiss. The response proved unanimous:

every person kissed back and expressed our sexual feelings for them back to us. Most of the men displayed other signs of excitement at our 'good morning' kiss. Eggs and tomatoes were banned in the kitchen after someone made an veggie omelet and both of us went running to the bathroom.

Eventually, everyone sat in some way in the kitchen or nearby family room area, all of us focused on each other and the planned events for the day.

Noah told us all, "There are two planned events for the day. First, two tee times at a nearby golf course occur in an hour. Who would like to play – raise your hands?"

Mark, Brad, Jeremy, Greg, David and Doug's hands went up instantly; Beth's hand rose. Noah said, "Okay, the eight of us should get ready to go now. We should be back by three o'clock. This will work out well because at four o'clock there is a special event that you should all be here for. In the meantime, please, no love making or sexing around."

A chorus of "What's going to happen?" and "Is someone coming?" echoed through the kitchen of the Villa, particularly from those of us that weren't going golfing. We were all curious about his secret.

Noah explained, "I won't tell you the details for what happens at four – and into the evening too, I might add, but you will want to save your sexual juices and erotic feelings. I guarantee you will all like what happens – even love it. By the way, you should be dressed casually at four."

Several in our group probed Noah for details but he was resolute in not providing any further information.

As Noah went up to change into his golfing clothes, I followed him. In our bedroom I locked him in a passionate embrace and pushed my pussy up his leg, begging for a quickie and information about what was going to happen.

Noah said stoically, "No sex. No further information." He gave me a sly little grin. He pushed me away from him, kissed me on the nose and sat me firmly on the bed. I pushed my lower lip out in a mock pout.

"You don't love me," I told him in a last futile attempt to elicit his secrets for the afternoon from him.

He finished dressing, came and kissed me on the nose again. He said, "I love you very much and will love you more than ever later and forever, in fact. Now you be a good golf widow and I'll see you later, Darling. Oh, yes, behave yourself." He disappeared. I followed along behind, but it was only to watch him join the others and see them disappear in the cars to the golf links.

Amy, Tiffany, Melissa, Alex, Jennifer and I congregated in the kitchen. They expected that I knew something about the four o'clock event. I didn't and it took a few minutes of intense grilling and persuasion before they believed I knew as little as they did.

Alex, Tiffany and Jennifer went off to the beach area in the nude to swim in the ocean and then relax around the lower pool. Melissa announced she was going to take a morning nap or read or both; she waddled off towards the living room with a paperback and I watched her curl up on the sofa and go right to sleep, her nude and pregnant body lying on its side in a way so her baby girl put the least pressure on any vital organs. I teared up now every time I looked at her swollen belly because my namesake was in there, just a few weeks from her arrival in this world. I started thinking if I'd look that good when I'm that pregnant.

Later, Amy and I went to the big pool and after finding some floats, set out to lounge around the pool. We took turns applying suntan lotion in liberal amounts to each of our bodies, we behaved ourselves.

The two of us had a talk, catching up on each other's lives. The difference from earlier times we'd seen each other was that now we had this new dimension that we could both talk about with each other, our sex lives. By the time we pulled our naked bodies from the pool, I was surprised the water hadn't boiled away. We had of both shared most of the significant sexual events in our lives and bonded with each other in a unique and erotic way that we had never done before.

"Details. Details. Details," Amy implored me. "Come on I want details about how this Caribbean Orgy all came to pass. Go back to day one!"

That was how we started, yet some of the stories and events I shared with her went back to when I lost my virginity in high school, a threesome I'd had several times with an old boyfriend, my Sapphic relationship with Alex, another threesome, meeting Ben, and then Noah all the various combinations I'd had over the past year leading up to this week on the Island.

Amy shared with me the details of a swing club she and a prior boyfriend had frequented, then her integration into a neighborhood in California where she ended up adopting a less lusty and more loving approach to her sex life, the latter providing a more satisfying set of relationships and feelings for her. We also talked about bisexuality and how it was different for women and men.

We talked about our values around relationships and sex and how they'd morphed over the years to where they were now. Somehow, quite independently of each other, we were pretty neutral on monogamy, believing we could each love more than one person at a time and, in fact, had or did. Further, neither of us wanted to be 'owned,' or to 'own' someone else; we wanted mature adult-adult relationships amongst equals. We both believed that our sexuality led to personal growth in many different ways and that we didn't think exclusivity supported our growth – we needed to be with other people in many different ways, including sexually.

"Life is too short to allow someone you feel you have chemistry with to pass by in an unfulfilled relationship," Amy told me; I agreed. "That said, I believe that sex is only one way to express your feelings and emotions for another person. These days the atmosphere has to be right, the ambience right, for me to get the most from hooking up with someone."

I chided her, "So is that why you got into the Mile High Club so quickly?" I shot her a teasing grin.

Amy laughed, "Well, to tell you the truth, every guy you hang around with turns me on. Maybe I'm lining up for sloppy seconds, but I think Doug and Brad are super and generous lovers, not to mention their wives. We were all in seventh heaven in the back of that plane as we romped around. Thank you for providing the forum for me to lose my high altitude virginity and to bond more deeply with everybody; I will forever be able to hold my head up high knowing I am a wellqualified member of the Club." She gave me a lecherous grin.

Amy and I fixed salads for everyone, leaving one covered for Melissa who still slept in the living room. We carried our lunch and those for the others down to the beach joining Alex, Tiffany and Jennifer. They were sitting in a triangle talking away when we arrived. They opened their circle to include us, and soon all of us launched into lunch and discussion of the major assets of the masseuses I'd arranged for the female members of the bridal party the morning of my wedding.

About two o'clock, I announced my short nap, carried the lunch dishes back to the house, and launched myself into the pool on my float again. I instantly slept awake about an hour later as I heard the cars pull into the driveway.

The golfers arrived full of good cheer and recounting various elements of their game, duffed shots, and questionable scoring. I got out of the pool and greeted them all, continuing to enjoy the long period of my daytime nudity. I'd have to remember to ask Noah about going to a nudist retreat sometime.

After a few minutes regrouping, Noah went down to the beach to herd the women down there back to the main house and into some clothes. I headed to our bedroom for a quick shower and some shorts and a colorful top. Noah joined me but carefully avoided physical contact with me as he showered and dressed. The lack of contact almost wound me up as tight as if we'd touched and teased each other, perhaps because it was so obvious an omission in our normal behavior.

One by one everyone joined us in the living room until all fourteen of us sat there looking at Noah. "Just be patient. We're to have a visitor I arranged. There is no part of this you won't enjoy and treasure for the rest of your lives. Our visitor will be here any moment, I'm sure."

We chatted until Doug heard a car in the driveway. "Someone's just arrived," he announced.

"I'll welcome our guest. Just wait here," Noah said to us all. He left the room and headed towards the front door of the Villa.

Chapter Twenty-Seven

I heard the door open then some greeting sounds and friendly conversation between Noah and a woman.

Joyous laughter came from the hallway.

Seconds later, Noah ushered a tall middle-aged Indian woman into the living room. She had long, jet black hair and nearly matching eyes beautifully set in her angular face. She carried herself in a stately manner and through her colorful sari I could see her magnificent figure.

Noah said, "I would like to introduce you all to Alyssa Patel. Please tell her your names as you greet her."

We'd all stood, and Alyssa went to Doug who was nearest the door. She stood facing him as he put his hand out in a greeting and told her, "I'm Doug."

Alyssa moved inside his outstretched arm and embraced him in a hug and kissed him on the left cheek. She said, "And I am Alyssa – your teacher and your new love." Doug looks puzzled.

Alyssa moved to Beth. She said, "I am Beth – Doug's wife." She too held her hand out in the very American form of greeting.

Alyssa moved inside her arm too and hugged Beth to her as she'd done before. "Beth, I am Alyssa – your teacher and your new love."

Alyssa repeated the process around the room until she'd completed our circle of fourteen. In the end she and Noah shared an even tighter embrace and kiss.

We all looked on with a great sense of puzzlement yet now stood awed by the impressive personality of this woman. Warmth and love emanated not only from her body but also from her very essence.

Noah motioned for us all to sit and we did. "You are all probably puzzled by Alyssa's presence with us. Alyssa is my guru, my teacher, and one of the first women in my life that I loved and still love with great devotion."

He locked eyes with me and I could tell by the smile and his laughing eyes that he had so much more to tell. Noah went on, "When I was twenty-two and just out of college I dated a girl who told me I needed to take up tantric sex if I ever expected to get to third base with her – let alone home plate. At the time I thought it might be an interesting endeavor and, as it turned out, I had a misguided idea of what tantric sex was all about. I was at a lusty age and the idea of infinitely long orgasms and bringing irresistible pleasures to your partner stimulated my interest." A few heads nodded in acknowledgement but not in understanding of where the afternoon was going.

He continued, "It turns out Tantra is so much more than some interesting sexual techniques. The process the way Alyssa taught me dealt with my holistic self – my Mind, Body and Spirit. I got these parts of my life in alignment and felt the richer for it."

Noah looked at me and smiled, "I've tried some of the techniques and things I remember on Avery, but I've forgotten so much I wanted a refresher. Further, as I got into graduate school and then my businesses, I got out of balance – way too much work and not enough attention to the other parts of my life.

Avery has restored some of that balance and I want to enter my new relationship with her with both of us balanced and complete individuals."

Noah continued. "We've proven beyond a doubt to each other that we are a very lusty and loving group of people - a fact I thank the Universe for every day. That said, however, I wanted Avery and me to start our marriage not only with a western view of our sexuality but also a deep appreciation of the philosophy and practices of tantric sex – a more eastern view of thing. I know from what I've learned it will make our lives more delicious and full of joy. Moreover I thought it might interest you so I invited Alyssa to come down to the Island and join us for a few days and play teacher as well as enjoy the Villa with us."

"I've heard of tantric sex but that's about all." Mark said. Several other heads nodded to indicate their same level of awareness.

"Tantra actually started about six-thousand years ago for many of the same reasons the protestant movement started in the western world in the 1500s," Alyssa spoke in her pure voice. "The religious movement that preceded it was corrupt, stifling, controlling, and had reached a point where it forbad sex for any reason other than procreation. Tantra re-launched a beautiful spirituality and embedded in it an appreciation of sex for procreation, for pleasure, and for spiritual connection with the Universe and your partner. The focus became completeness for the individual in terms of Mind, Body and Spirit."

"The balance I spoke of a moment ago is a journey not an end point. Tantric sex is much the same. As I found some sort of Mind, Body and Spiritual balance, I also found I became a better lover," Noah stepped in again. "I produced more pleasure for my dates and for myself, made the right things last longer, and eliminated inessentials. I could be more genuine and intimate in my relationships and found new and exciting meaning in those couplings. I was a better person and now I need to re-ground myself in some of those fundamentals.

"Alyssa, tell us about what you'll teach us this week, if we're lucky," Noah spoke softly.

"Based on what Noah has told me about you and your passionate times together, I believe you would like to find out how to extend and even heighten the pleasure you give and derive from each other. In the short time I can spend with you I will show you some techniques, however, this area is about energy management, sexual energy management by your conscious and unconscious mind," Alyssa paused and assessed our circle; "Through this teaching I will bring you my own perspectives on energy, balance and spirituality, and how they too enhance our sexuality and the connectedness we feel with one another and with the Universe. We will only scratch the surface this week."

"I find this fascinating and ... well, how do we start?" Tiffany asked.

"Please, everyone, sit forward on the edge of your seat back straight, eyes open and alert," Alyssa said and took a chair Noah brought for her.

There was a shuffling around the room as we shifted towards the front of our chairs or the sofa. Even Melissa, heavy with child, levered herself up and to the edge of the chair she'd claimed. Alyssa continued, "First, I want you to breath from deep inside you, from your chest then you're your abdomen and then from your sexual organs." The room filled with the sound of deep breathing. "Now, slowly engage in eye contact with another. Be quiet. Just talk through your eyes. Don't spend more than a minute or so in contact with any one person."

I locked eyes with Jennifer, and we smiled and held each other's gaze for a while. I broke off and moved until Amy and I made eye contact. Several more times I shifted and had contact with my friends. After about ten minutes of observing us and occasionally participating, Alyssa said, "What did you feel in each of these transactions?"

"I wanted to make a deeper connection this seemed too superficial. By the way, the baby liked the deep breaths; she kicked a lot," Melissa said.

"I wanted to know what the person was thinking, sometimes about me but also just in general," Brad spoke.

"I wanted some physical contact with the person," Beth commented.

"I sensed different moods in people but realized I'd made up a story about each person and what they were thinking," I said.

Several others shared similar comments about the hollow nature of the connections yet acknowledged that there had been a connection of some sort.

"Now I want you to hold the person's hands as you look into their eyes, make physical contact and this time hold each person's eyes for five minutes or more. Initially choose someone other than your regular partner. Go ahead, restart," Alyssa said.

I recalled several times Noah and I had done this, staring into each other's eyes for long time periods. Each time my heart gushed with love and affection for him; he told me he'd felt the same way.

Jeremy and I teamed up. We pulled our chairs to face each other and leaned forward in them holding hands. As we looked into each other's eyes I felt an overwhelming feeling of love for him and for the world. I went through a minute or so of sadness and cried, the tears streaming down my face; Jeremy cried too. We ignored our tears. I felt passion for him. I sent him messages of love and caring. I felt embraced and almost closer to Jeremy than any other human being.

We continued to look into each other's eyes. I became aware of a connection and closeness I'd never felt before. The world faded away and there were only Jeremy's eyes and my feelings of love – yes, sexual love, and also brotherly love, familial love, devotion and awe.

Alyssa called us all back to 'class' with a loud "Ahem. Please finish your thoughts and rejoin us."

Jeremy and I reluctantly broke off our contact with the other.

"How much time has passed since we started this exercise?" Alyssa asked. After several guesses Alyssa informed us that about twenty minutes had gone by. I'd become oblivious of time. "Are any of you sure about what your partner was thinking?"

Each of us raised our hands. "I felt certain that the thoughts of love, happiness, sharing, physical lust, sorrow and enlightenment I'd felt had come from Jeremy." I said.

"Verify with each other that what you felt and the messages you received are in fact accurate," Alyssa requested softly in her smooth voice.

I explained to Jeremy what I'd found in my head. He validated that we were aligned and thinking the same things.

Overall we expressed our love for each other.

As the room silenced, "You see if you focus on your partner you reach a new level of exchange, of communication, of unity, of connection," Alyssa said.

Heads nodded around the room on the profundity of this simple lesson. Alyssa went on, "Now imagine the connection you could make if you spent a longer time and were nude and sexually connected. What would that be like?"

"I'm not sure I could stand it," I volunteered after the room was silent to her question. "I mean that would be a wonderful and deep connection but it'd be so revealing of my own mind."

"What were you all doing as you looked at each other?" Alyssa said to my statement.

"Just looking and touching," Beth offered. "Otherwise, just being."

"Good," Alyssa said. "You were 'being' without 'acting.' Taking action gets in the way of feeling." She paused and asked, "Were any of you judging?"

"In the first minute or two, yes, but then less and less," Tiffany said tentatively. Tiffany and Mike Lafontaine had been partners for the exercise. He nodded in agreement with her statement.

"Judgments prevent you from enjoying the present moment. You become too wrapped up in whether you are right or wrong, whether you like or don't like what is happening, what other people might think of you or what you're doing, and on and on. If you can suspend your judgments you feel the present moment the way it really is," Alyssa told us "without opinions or shading."

"Sometimes I asked myself if I'd felt this way with Brad or Noah or someone else," Jennifer said.

"So, you made comparisons to earlier situations? Did anyone else?" Alyssa asked.

A few heads nodded.

"When you bind yourself to the past by comparing what you are feeling now with a past 'then', you rob yourself of the ability to find a new feeling in the new experience," Alyssa spoke. "Each experience has the potential to be new if you let it. New experience, new ideas, new possibilities versus the past. What sounds more exciting to you?"

Again we saw the points she raised to us.

"Why have sex with each other? What is your goal?" Alyssa asked us.

"An orgasm," Greg stated. "Feeling good when the climax arrives."

A few heads nodded agreement.

"You start a sexual situation with a goal in mind...the orgasm. What happens if you don't have that peak experience?" Alyssa asked us.

"I feel inadequate. I failed my partner and I failed myself. I don't like to be robbed of that pleasure," Greg answered her.

"Ah, there's some pleasure involved!" Alyssa chided with a smile. She asked further, "Can you have some pleasure without the orgasm?"

"Yes, of course. The foreplay, teasing, dancing, kissing, romance, talking, storytelling, smoothing, licking, sucking, blowing, feeling and whatever else I forgot all help make the experience feel good...pleasurable," Melissa said.

"Good," Alyssa said. "What role do expectations have in what you feel?"

"If I go into a love making session expecting how it'll be, I can end up disappointing myself. If I don't have expectations, I'm often pleasantly surprised with the way things turn out," Greg answered again.

"So your focus on the future on expectations you can rob yourself of enjoyment of the present?" Alyssa asked.

Most of us nodded in agreement.

She said, "So here, in less than an hour you have learned four lessons that deal with the obstacles to good sex and that pave the way to enjoying what some call tantric sex. First, just be live in the 'now.'" Alyssa began "Second, do not judge...take the pleasure as it comes. Third, leave the past behind. Fourth, do not have expectations about the future. This is all about the journey and enjoying the process as it unfolds before you." We all looked expectantly at her.

"While I explore your beautiful Villa, please each of you pair with your partners. Please go, get naked, join in a sexual way but do not talk and do not orgasm. Can we meet here again in ninety minutes," Alyssa said. "Noah tells me we will then go into the town for dinner so please come dressed casually."

"We have two large tables reserved at a seafood restaurant for eight o'clock. We'll have time for a few cocktails and some discussion here before we go," Noah stepped forward and said.

We paired off. Alyssa suggested that Mark go with Tiffany since they were recently married. Melissa waddled off with Mike Lafontaine. Greg and Amy became a pair as well. The rest of us went with our spouses.

Noah and I went to our room in silence. When I attempted to suggest something, Noah gently put his fingers on my lips to silence me. I smiled at him and got the message. We both pulled each other's clothing from our bodies. Noah sat in the middle of the bed and I sucked on him briefly to get him to requisite hardness to penetrate me. I nestled into his lap and together we worked his hard cock into my vagina. Then, unlike the times we'd tried to fuck each other silly, we just rested and looked into each other's eyes for a while then looked and visually explored each other's bodies and faces.

We smiled and even laughed a few minutes into this exercise, much as I had with Jeremy an hour earlier. Gradually, we settled down and just stared into our eyes and then into our very souls. We often moved and writhed into each other in a very sexual way. Noah often pumped his cockhead back and forth along my tunnel, and we often smoothed and touched each other in a sensuous way.

I felt an amazing thing happen as our hour progressed. I grew closer and closer to Noah. Soon I knew he could not only read my every thought and mood, but also what I felt. I mirrored exactly what he was thinking and vice versa; we'd become synchronized, loving beings. I grew closer to Noah and knew, instinctively, that the love was deep, real, and profoundly sensuous. I became amazed at how close I could feel to Noah without a single word being spoken.

We shared a quick shower in our bathroom, slipped on our clothing again, and went downstairs. As we got to the bottom stair I said to Noah in a whisper, "Can we talk now?"

"Yes, Darling," Noah whispered and kissed the side of my head.

"I just want you to know that I loved what we just did and I feel so close to you. I feel like we saw into each other's souls. In this past hour," I said. "I feel so close to you. Almost like I've seen parts of you I never knew existed and I love them all."

Chapter Twenty-Eight

We stood and snuggled in the hallway for a few minutes, cooing intimate words of love to each other.

Eventually, I heard noises from above signaling that others were ending their exercises. I felt a domestic wave sweep over me. I turned to Noah, "I'm going to fix some hors d'oeuvres. Can you play host to Alyssa?"

Ben headed off to the pool deck. I could see Alyssa's naked body sitting in the classic lotus position astride a lounger beside the pool, her back towards the house. She faced out over the magnificent Caribbean. I paused to watch Noah gently touch her shoulder. She responded with a turn to him and a smile. I watched with pleasure as Alyssa reached up and pulled Noah into a tender kiss before she uncoiled her lithe body to stand nude beside him. Her body really was magnificent, her dark toned skin giving her a healthy look we all aspired to.

I had laid out some cheeses, crackers and a few other nibbles when Noah and Alyssa joined me in the spacious kitchen.

Alyssa remained nude. "Where do you live?" I asked politely of Alyssa.

"I reside in San Diego. I grew up and received my education near Agra. The site of the Taj Mahal. My mentor still resides there, and we talk frequently thanks to modern technology."

I turned to Noah. "How did you meet? This is a side of you I never knew."

The two laughed. Noah said, "When I wanted the tantric training a friend recommended Alyssa to me. She had just come to the United States then. I called and the next thing I knew I became her student and her lover. I trained in yoga, tantric sex, life balance and spirituality, Hinduism and relationships. I invested about sixteen weeks over that first year." He paused and went on, "I know you haven't seen much evidence of these areas in our relationship so far. As I said when I introduced Alyssa, I've reverted to western ways so this is a good refresher for me again. I've forgotten so much I didn't think to mention the specific trips and training to you. I didn't mean to hide anything from you; well, at least until I got the idea to invite Alyssa down here."

Greg and Amy joined us and right behind them Mike and Melissa. Noah poured wine for us. The new arrivals just sat close together in obvious affection for one another and listened to our conversation. "You drink?" I asked Alyssa, perhaps with a surprised tint to my voice.

"Oh, yes," she laughed. "I've become pretty westernized and I'm not a purist. If I have one focus, it is joy. Wine is a joy for me, often. As are many other things in this world. Life is not about denial of pleasures; it is about awareness and appreciation."

"Why didn't you invite her to the wedding?" I asked.

"Noah called seven weeks ago about whether I could come to the wedding. I had to be in India for a month up through the past weekend so regrettably I could not attend," Alyssa smiled at Noah and spoke, "As we talked Noah and I thought up my joining you for your honeymoon and doing some teaching. He assured me you would all welcome this and he wanted it to be a surprise.

Don't feel rejected because of my secret," Noah said to me. "I wanted to surprise you and everyone else. For years after my initial work with Alyssa this training helped me so. I've felt a hole in my thinking as I've become aware of how I've lost touch with the training and its application."

"Oh, no," I said. "I think this is wonderful. Keep surprising me like this." I turned to Alyssa and said, "The one hour we spent together. I haven't felt as close to Noah as I do now. I should tell you that over our marriage I look forward to the unraveling of the mysteries we each hold inside us. As each of these mysteries is revealed, our intimacy and love will deepen."

Ben's sisters and their husbands arrived downstairs, closely followed by Jeremy and Alex.

"I'm in love again – with Melissa," David volunteered, "I don't know that I've ever felt so close to another human in my life."

"I feel the same way about Greg." Amy sighed aloud, reaching and squeezing his hand.

"I'm feeling the same about Amy," Greg said.

Doug and Beth joined us completing the group. They both were hugging one another as they appeared in the room.

"The feelings of love, attraction and closeness you feel for each other are the normal response from the exercise you did. You can repeat the exercise with others that are as attuned as you are to each other and to the obstacles to tantrism," Alyssa said, "The ones we discussed before you went off with each other. Did you all have a nice experience?"

"The best in my life," Tiffany said softly; she reached out and stroked Mark's bare arm in a caring and affectionate gesture. Her response and attitude surprised me. I thought she might be the one amongst us to least appreciate tantric sex.

"Beth and I have been married ten years and we went together three years before that," Doug said. "In all that time, I never thought I'd attain the closeness I felt with her like I did over the past hour." He wrapped his arms around Beth and kissed the top of her head.

"Tantric sex is a way of thinking about yourself and your partner or partners. It is spiritual and if you go into a coupling with a spiritual mindset you should have an experience of enlightenment. Tomorrow we will talk about this. Tonight I want you to change partners and repeat the experience you shared." Alyssa laughed, "Only this time, after the hour, you may complete the orgasm if you both are so inclined. I recommend you keep your conversation to a minimum as well as the urge to do anything fast, including breathing. Take it all slow do not rush to orgasm."

"Based on what I know I would choose your partners for later now, because the 'dance' we are to do starts immediately and carries into the night," Noah added.

"I need to be with Melissa, to share this experience with my other wife." Mark smiled warmly at her as she moved to his side, her pregnant belly pushing into his side. He smiled at the intrusion as he hugged her.

"Now mix this up and bit and pick someone else," Alyssa said.

The other couplings were announced through eye contact or verbal announcement: Greg and Alex; Doug and Tiffany; Jennifer and Jeremy; David and Beth; Amy and Noah; and Brad and me.

I realized we were all couples except for Alyssa. "What about you?" I asked her. "Will you come and join us?"

Alyssa looked at me with an aura of love and almost a halo of spirituality around her, "Yes, I will," she said. She turned to some of the others and added, "I may join all of you in some way." She picked up her sari and started to re-dress, showing no shyness for her nudity amongst our clothed bodies.

Chapter Twenty-Nine

At dinner, Alyssa had us hand feed each other, encouraging us to touch each other's faces and lips in the process. "Tantric sex is about sensual feelings and the spirituality we'll talk about tomorrow. Lips and fingers are two of many sensual points of the body and should be used both to give and receive enjoyment."

I leaned in and fed Alyssa a small tidbit of cheese. She looked deep and lovingly into my eyes. "You are a deep and loving person, Avery. Thank you for the care and love you have about the Universe."

I started a trend. I went around the tables and fed each person and followed each ceremony with a kiss. With many I used my tongue to caress their lips and touch deep inside their mouth. I noticed the waitress watch me as I circulated. As I took my place again, I again fed Alyssa and kissed the older woman. As we parted I said, "Thank you for being the Spiritual Being you are."

Alyssa smiled at me and said, "You are more Spiritual than you realize, Avery. You will see deeper into your own soul as we move through this process."

"How do you know?" I asked her, confused by her statement.

"I am Spirit," Alyssa said. "We are all connected and you and I share a connection as you will discover before long." She ran her tongue around my lips in a highly sensuous move and then we parted.

I glanced around the restaurant. Our waitress stood a few feet from us. She looked at me and our glances caressed each other. I smiled warmly at her; she smiled back. Alyssa urged moderation in our consumption of alcohol. "You will be a better lover and respond better without too much liquor in your system, men especially," she told us. She also urged us to avoid red meats and fatty foods for the same reason. "These foods and many others capture your body for a long time and do not allow the release and pleasure you hope for. Your mind is lugged down and does not work as smoothly."

She also urged us to do little things for each other and to touch each other frequently. "Come up with a fantasy you'd like to explore with your new partner. Make them the star of that fantasy and then tell them, even do it with them." Alyssa glanced around the restaurant with a worried expression on her face and we all laughed at her humor.

Around the table I noticed a number of whispered conversations and often smiles and kisses as each couple communicated with each other. Brad told me quietly about wanting to take me on a luxury yacht, anchoring off shore so we could see the beauty of the Island from the water, and then spending the day making love to me in a thousand different ways and positions. He graphically described what he would like to do to me. Shivers started in my womb and radiated up my body.

I felt myself getting wet in anticipation.

I told Brad I would like to sneak into his office and get under his desk where I could proceed to perform oral sex on him all day long as his colleagues came and went in his office with none of them aware of what was happening. As I told him, I stroked his legs; I could visually verify that he found my fantasy exciting.

After dinner we drove back to the villa in the cars we'd used to drive into the town. Those not driving cuddled and stroked each other the way teenagers often do when on a first date. At the Villa, Noah volunteered liqueurs to anyone interested. Brad poured Grand Marnier, took a sip and then went to

Alyssa. He bent to kiss her red lips and she entered the kiss with him. I watched as he thrust his tongue into her mouth and then jetted the sweet liqueur into her. She flowed with the experience, and I could watch her savoring not only the liqueur but also Brad's affection.

As they parted Alyssa said to Brad, "That is a very sexy and sensuous thing to do. I hope you have taught that to the others." Brad nodded. She went on, "Thank you, my Love, for teaching me. The teacher always learns from the students." She caressed his face as she leaned in and kissed him again.

Unlike the prior evenings, each couple gradually left the group and disappeared to their quarters, often hand in hand. Brad eventually led me to his room. Jennifer stood nude in the room with Jeremy. I went and kissed both of them then we left to find unoccupied space.

Noah was not evident in our bedroom, so Brad and I claimed our bed for the night. Brad and I opened the doors to the upper veranda and enjoyed the warmth of the evening and the onshore breezes. We took over fifteen minutes to remove each other's clothing, our kisses covered the newly bared skin as we disposed of each piece.

Standing nude before each other Brad allowed me to give him a nipple massage. I writhed around him, my erect nipples dragging across his body in hundreds of different ways. I pushed him onto the bed and used my nipples to caress and touch his erection. Occasionally I would lick and then blow on his rod to add sensation to his experience. Brad took the lead and stroked me all over with his hardness on my breasts, arms, around my face, ears, neck, thighs, stomach and my pubic area.

He carefully avoided my vagina for the time being.

I assumed Alyssa had wanted us to be more inventive in our lovemaking so as Brad's cock passed my lips I mouthed the mushroomed head and then urged him to stroke into my mouth. Per her instructions, we kept things slow and I took my time loving his rod, first directly from the end and then almost like I was eating corn on the cob. I also loved his scrotum. Brad knelt next to me on the bed and we allowed ourselves a long time in our cock play.

Brad finally pulled away from me and stretched out next to me. He made love to my breasts, one at a time, not only bringing my nipples back to full ripeness but also loving over the whole of each taut globe. Then he made love to my navel, running his tongue in and out of the knotted hole.

At last he reached my pubic area, his tongue darting around my upper thighs and around my narrow strip of pubic hair. He worked his way closer and closer to my vagina and my clitoris, occasionally allowing his tongue to catch a droplet of my generous secretions.

"Are we allowed to have orgasms other than at the end?" he asked.

"I don't see why not. I just think she didn't want a 'wham bam thank you mam' kind of fuck."

"Then relax and let me bring you even more pleasure," Brad whispered.

His head nestled back into my groin, his tongue slowly stroking my sweet spot and often penetrating the first couple of inches of my tunnel. I flowed juices and just as fast Brad licked them from me. He praised my taste and texture.

Two fingers penetrated my tunnel and immediately found the clitoral sponge or G-spot. I relaxed into the feelings of pleasure that swept over me, reminding myself to enjoy the sensation without rushing to orgasm.

Nonetheless, the orgasm found me. I reached down and pressed Brad's head to my throbbing cunt as the climax swept through me. I could feel the warmth of the event start deep within my lower abdomen and radiate outward in successive seismic waves. I know I gave a loud moan of appreciation to my lover.

After I relaxed from my tremors, Brad kissed his way up my body and embraced my face in his hands.

"Avery, I love you dearly. I would move heaven and earth to bring you pleasure," Brad said.

"Thank you, dear lover. I love you and feel the same. You are a divine lover. I am so glad we can share these moments with one another." As we kissed, I became aware of a third person in the room beside the bed. We turned and Alyssa stood there, her naked body a wonder to behold.

"You two are beautiful to watch," Alyssa said. "You are excellent students of keeping things slow and measured in your lovemaking."

"Did you watch us?" I asked.

"Yes, at least for the past five minutes or so. I watched Brad's cunnilingus – excellent, as well as your use of tongue and fingers to stimulate and arouse. I like how you only talk to each other in measured tones and words as well," Alyssa stated.

We both nodded to her. Brad turned more fully to see her beside us. Alyssa knelt on the bed beside him. She reached to his erect penis and slowly stroked the rod. I could see him harden further at the unexpected touches from her.

"May I have Brad make love to me as well?" Alyssa asked softly. The very thought excited me greatly. I nodded my assent.

Alyssa slowly masturbated Brad's long rod, the head now a tone of purple with arousal and need for release. She brought her mouth to his shaft and pushed her head completely down until his cock completely disappeared down her throat. Her head bobbed slowly as she repeated the gesture over and over for a minute. Brad's head was thrown back in his ecstasy.

Suddenly she pulled off of him and I could see her reach and squeeze his cock with her hand. Brad let out a long sigh and moan.

"You had an orgasm?" she asked Brad.

He speechlessly nodded vigorously in her general direction, clearly still awash in the flow of pleasure through his body.

"No fluids. He didn't ejaculate. Just as you can cum over and over again, and even get up on the step in one infinitely long orgasm, a man can too. In this case, I prevented his ejaculation, but he can do it through concentration and self-discipline," She turned to me and said.

Brad looked at me with a helpless expression that shifted to a smile. "That was wonderful, and I can still make love."

"Brad, please make love to me," Alyssa said. Brad looked at me for approval. I nodded encouragingly.

I joined Brad and together we made love to Alyssa. I caressed and loved her face and upper body as Brad repeated his tAllents on her cunt. Soon enough Alyssa moaned her approvals to us and urged us to further endeavors on her behalf. Brad and I traded places so he could romance her and I could taste Alyssa's fluids.

Alyssa came in a soft orgasm as I ministered to her. She just announced to us, "I'm cuming, right now. Oh, thank you. Such a wonderful feeling you've given me." She sighed several times. "I would like you to have intercourse with me. Please Brad, penetrate me and love me."

Brad and I moved to change places but, to my surprise, Brad scooped up the beautiful Indian woman and carried her across the bedroom and through the doors onto the upper veranda. A large lounger faced the dark Caribbean and the night sky just outside the door.

He carefully set Alyssa down on the lounger and moved between her legs, his penis more erect than ever. I stood in the doorway and watched as he penetrated her just enough to bury the mushroomed head in her folds. She reached up and stroked his chest.

Brad pulled out the short distance of his penetration and slowly re-entered her folds, this time moving infinitesimally deeper into her body. He paused and withdrew, the purple head of his cock glistening with her juices and waving in the dim light from the pool and outdoor lights.

He again positioned at the entrance to her vagina and pushed into her, this time moving only slightly deeper than his prior did. He withdrew. Alyssa moaned her approval at his approach. She held her arms open to me and I went and lay beside the two lovers in the three-person lounger.

Brad again withdrew, paused, and penetrated again, moving only a fraction deeper than his earlier thrust. He repeated and repeated this move, never in a rush to bottom out, not acquiescing to urge to wildly pound into Alyssa's velvet cunt.

After many minutes, Brad finally bottomed out. The two lovers ground their hips into one another as their organs enjoyed the pleasure of a complete union.

Alyssa whispered to Brad, "Just pump slowly into me. Make me enjoy your thrusts as much as you do. When you feel the urge to cum I want you to stop and back down from that urge. Do that twice then cum in me."

As I held Alyssa and kissed her beautiful face and breasts, Brad pumped into her at an even and measured pace. I felt him stop and looked at him in the shadows. He watched the two of us with a halo of love. He leaned across the lounger and kissed Alyssa and then kissed me, delivering a shower of tender kisses. He rose again and re-started his thrusts.

Minutes later he again moved in and showered the two of us with kisses. As he returned to his thrusting Alyssa whispered to me, "Please put your pussy against my mouth. I want to taste you and bring you pleasure."

I shifted around on the lounger holding on to the edge as I carefully backed over her face. Alyssa's tongue immediately found my soft spot and then thrust upward into my vagina. I jerked with the arrival of her pleasure, amazed at how in two seconds she'd found my trigger points as though she'd known ahead of time.

My juices started to flow again as her tongue lapped at my cunt. I could feel the thrusts of Brad into her body and often his hands as he stroked my back and buttocks. "I feel another orgasm coming," I whispered to my lovers.

From beneath me, Alyssa instructed, "Avery, cum. Pleasure yourself on my tongue, on my face." I felt her fingers thrust into me occasionally, pulling fluids from my body onto her tongue."

I allowed myself to drift and then fell into the maelstrom of an orgasm, writhing almost out of control as the joy again started deep in my body and swelled to my groin, thighs and breasts. I almost blacked out at the pleasure as I froze in position above her face. Somehow I managed to lie beside Alyssa and allow her to embrace me. Brad had paused as I came and now thrust again into the lovely, exotic Alyssa.

I felt Brad speed up slightly. Alyssa encouraged his more rapid thrusts and then suddenly there were a half dozen major long thrusts into each other's bodies as the pair climaxed into each other. Both mewled softly and then whispered love words to each other and to me. I shifted to hold Alyssa in her after glow. Brad gently lowered himself onto us and again kissed us and told us of his love. We remained like that for a long time before Brad moved and shifted behind Alyssa as we sandwiched her between us. Our hands continued to smooth, and our mouths continued to kiss and speak of love.

Alyssa left us eventually, pushing Brad and my nude bodies together in a further gesture of love and caring. We slept on the comfortable lounger, the soft breezes of the Caribbean caressing our warm bodies.

Chapter Thirty

I awoke cradled in Brad's arms. My eyes blinked open to the dawn light rising on the other side of the Villa and sweeping across the sea. I lay and enjoyed the comfort of Brad's arms and the closeness I felt to him. As I looked down the porch I saw two other couples out on the veranda as well: Jeremy and Jennifer, and Greg and Alex. Alex slowly gyrated above Greg's body as they made love. The other couple seemed to be asleep.

"They're beautiful, aren't they?" Brad whispered in my ear. He'd awoken and been watching as well.

"They are. I never tire of watching people make love, especially people I love," I said.

We watched until Alex had an obvious orgasm freezing in position above Greg's arched form. I somehow suspected that the lessons Alyssa had been trying to impart to us the evening before had been temporarily forgotten by the duo.

We heard two splashes from below. I slipped away from Brad and peered over the balcony. Tiffany and Doug drifted along the length of the pool under water, their nude forms visible beneath the surface.

At the shallow end of the pool Mark was helping Melissa negotiate the stairs into the pool. The care he displayed showed an obvious love and caring for his pregnant partner. Even from above I could see the stretch marks across Melissa's swollen belly.

"Brad, come let's join the others in the pool or even swim in the ocean." I pulled Brad to his feet and we walked through our room to the stairs. Seconds later we dove into the pool and greeted the others with kisses.

"Did you make love?" I asked Melissa. "Can you make love?" I smoothed her breasts and abdomen with one hand.

"Oh, yes," Melissa said. "Just because I'm two thousand months pregnant doesn't mean I can't fuck. We were gentle and Mark is a divine lover – very caring and careful about me. I feel pampered by him. Just thinking about last night makes me flow and tingle all over."

Jeremy and Jennifer joined us from the shallow end, gliding into the pool water with smiles and then hugs and kisses for everyone. Greg and Alex followed Noah and Amy, all giving out similar greetings to everyone. Finally, David and Beth appeared, blushing as they were the last to join our circle; I took the blush to mean they'd been in a sexual romp only moments earlier. Both looked rosy and had a glow about them.

"Where's Alyssa?" I asked as I looked around the circle.

Noah looked at me and shrugged, his rugged figure and manly physique amplified by his nudity. Melissa shook her head, as did Tiffany.

"She spent two or three hours with us last night," Doug volunteered.

"And with us," Noah said.

"And with us," Brad and David simultaneously.

Puzzled looks went around the circle in the pool.

Greg said slowly, "I know she was at least an hour with us, probably longer."

Jennifer added even more slowly, "And we made love with her for a couple of hours too."

"There aren't that many hours in the night. How could we all have spent so much time with her?" I asked.

"She is magical. She can do things none of us dream about. It's part of who she is and how she teaches," Noah said softly.

I took the descending stairs from the pool telling the others over my shoulder, "I'll look for her down on the beach." I took the stone stairs down to the beach and the lower pool. The shaded area was cooler than the areas the sun was now starting to reach. The cool sand felt good against my feet.

Alyssa sat naked on a beach towel, her legs entwined in the lotus position and her arms extended over her knees. Her thumbs and fingers formed small circles. Her meditative state and motionless body gave her a surreal look; for a moment I thought I could actually see an aura around her sensual body.

Without looking at me she raised her arms and stretched, extending her arms towards the water's edge. Her legs unfurled and she extended her body in a long stretch across each leg.

"Good morning, Avery," she said to me before she turned and looked at me for the first time that morning.

"I just wondered where you were. We all did," I said as I walked up to her.

Without asking she closed the distance between us, and we shared a loving embrace and kiss. Her lips tasted like a sweet wine delicious and pliant in their response to me.

"Good morning, Love," she told me more intimately.

"Thank you for coming to see us last night. Apparently you visited all of, but we can't figure out how you spent so much time with all of us over the short night," I said.

Alyssa gave me an enigmatic smile as she picked up her towel and the two of us started walking towards the stairs. She never responded to my comment.

Chapter Thirty-One

The others greeted Alyssa, often with kisses and hugs. I heard the question of her impossible visits raised by a couple of people but never heard an answer just silence as she dove into the pool and washed away the past.

Noah, Amy and I made breakfast for everyone. The well-stocked kitchen provided sufficient stock for omelets all around for those that ate. Brad, Beth and David did clean up duty. We seemed to work well together and for the most part our nudity did not act as a deterrent, only a visual stimulant to us all.

As clean up ended, Noah announced that Alyssa would continue the lessons starting at ten o'clock in the living room, but that attendance was optional now that she'd been introduced. He made it clear he didn't want to force her or the accompanying philosophy on anyone.

An hour later all fourteen of us were seated in the living room. We remained nude. Several couples sat close, wrapped in the arms of their morning partner.

Alyssa came into the room clothed only in a thin sari that was sexy and revealing.

"Thank you for all being here," Alyssa started. "This afternoon we will revisit the lessons from the night, however, now I feel like talking about our Spirit. Please relax. Be comfortable with your partner or partners." I could feel some of the tension in the room deflating immediately.

Alyssa went on, "I use the term 'our Spirit' because I believe we share a Spirit force with one another. On a non-physical plane we are as one, connected and joined, at one with each other and with the same God-force that flows through everything everywhere."

"We are much like waves on an ocean. The ocean is what we are made of and that to which we belong. We are not separate from the ocean except in the brief individuality each of us have as a wave," Alyssa began again. "I believe the God force is all there is. We live, move and have our being in the mind of God. This physical world is our creation, much as a wave is created. There are no other forces in the Universe; no devil, no demons, no ogres, except as we create with our minds. We create our own reality."

"We are Spiritual Beings having a human experience. We created this situation for ourselves and our purpose here is to grow, evolve and experience joy and bliss. The latter being our natural state unless we do something to reject and change that state. Any heaven or hell exists here and now and is of our own creation. We always have the option of free will and the self-determinism of our thoughts and actions," Alyssa paused looked around, she began again. "Putting this in more human terms, if you want to change your life, change your thinking. One author put it another way, 'There is nothing good or bad, but thinking makes it so.' You have the ability to see the worst of a good situation or the best of a bad situation, but you are the deciding factor."

"Thus, as part of the God force and together with the God force, we each co-create our own lives. We blend and move together in that accepting and harmonious Universe, our energies moving and blending with the others we share these dimensions with," Alyssa stopped and looked around the room. "Now questions," she invited. The discussion started and she was smooth and adept in how she responded regarding the basis of her philosophy.

"How does this relate to the tantric sex lessons from yesterday and last night?" Doug asked.

"Tantrism is really a Mind-Body-Spirit connection. Noah told me you all had the 'body' part down pretty well." She smiled at all of us and a ripple of laughter ran through the room. "What you may want to consider is a Transformation. There are so many other dimensions to your sexuality. Besides the lust and orgasm, your sexuality is a pathway to enlightenment and a bridge between the human and the divine," Alyssa began. "Tantric sex is about building and harmonizing the connection between Mind, Body and Spirit. Balance and activity in each area flows with an active energy to the other areas. As most of you experienced last night, your use of your intellectual abilities in figuring out how to please each other led to wonderful experiences."

Heads nodded in agreement around the room.

"The better the sex, the more your mind surged with that energy. At the same time you felt the greater oneness with your partner, even when it wasn't your primary life partner you still felt the spiritual bond start to form," Alyssa continued looking around the room. "If you understand the Spirit and your relation to that God force, you can heighten even further the flow of energy into your relationships and your sexual couplings. You understand sexual energy and body power or energy. Now understand Spiritual energy. You can funnel each to the other and amplify all that you are, have or do without limit." She gestured to us for more questions and a more open discussion prevailed. Suddenly it was one o'clock.

"Before we break for lunch, I want each of you to spend an hour or more after lunch meditating. I don't mean sleeping, just to be clear. Please go to a quiet place by yourself, sit comfortably, and free your mind of all thought. You will each find this difficult; I suspect. Listen for a small voice from within and see what you find. We will re-convene at four o'clock," Alyssa dismissed us with a short challenge.

Over lunch, several of us peppered Alyssa with questions about 'meditation' and how to do it correctly. The statement I remember; "There is no right or wrong way to meditate. Just go and do it in your own way and in your own place."

I put on bikini bottoms as a token adherence to propriety on the public beach, took my watch and towel, and walked a couple of hundred yards down the beach to a dune that looked out over the sea. I spread out a towel and sat, realizing I could not force my legs into a lotus position. I just hugged my knees and looked out at the water, initially focusing on a large sailboat a mile off shore that had captured the wind and now raced through the ocean.

At first, I found it hard to tune out the chatter in my head. My thoughts kept whirling around. Persistently I focused on nothing ... and then on everything in the Universe all at once. My mind alternated between expansion and total inclusion and contraction and narrowing to the small sliver of sail near the horizon.

I listened for the message – a message from within ... then from anywhere. Was there a message? Did I already know the answers to the unasked questions?

I re-lived the experiences of the past few weeks, particularly my life with Ben and Noah. I loved them but Ben didn't love me. He felt bad that Noah went with me more than the fact that I left him. I have a new life inside of me and I thought Ben would be happy but no, he wasn't, Noah loves me and wants this child even if it's not his.

I love all my friends. I knew they loved me. I knew I loved all of humanity in that instant as well. The thoughts exploded in a sea of rainbows and fireworks, a mental orgasm without physical stimulation or sexual involvement. I felt a unity with each person I loved a connectedness again. My thoughts vanished and only the sailboat remained canted in the wind as it tacked towards its island home.

I walked back into the warm Caribbean sun feeling a unique peace and filled with love. I met Alex coming from the other direction as we made our way beach house, we hugged and walked up the stone steps arm in arm. Strangely we didn't speak to one another.

Alex and I went to the living room and sat close to one another; she put her arms around me and we just sat. Doug came in alone and then the others started to drift in one by one. Alyssa came in wearing her sexy sari again.

Without waiting for full attendance, Alyssa asked, "How do you feel? What was your time alone like? Avery, why don't you start? The others will join us as they finish their meditations."

I described my feeling of love and peace as well as my focus on the sailboat. I talked about the feel of my focus expanding and contracting, as well as the feeling of wellness and wholeness. I told the group that meditating had been a challenge because I seldom felt my mind wasn't active and fighting my attempts at 'blankness'.

The others described similar experiences with only a few variations. Alex surprised me by also commenting on her focus on the same sailboat off the Island's shore.

By the time we finished going around the circle and discussing our experiences, the rest of our circle had joined us and it was six o'clock. Alyssa took the lead again in charting our evening. "I again want you each to choose a different person for this evening's pairings again, preferably not your spouse or regular partner. Tonight, I want you to love your partners remembering all we've talked about for the past twenty-four hours." Alyssa started to reiterate our lessons on her fingers, "Put the emphasis on 'being' not 'doing'; suspend judgments about what you're doing or what others might ever think about it; focus on the now and don't bring the past or expectations for the future into your lovemaking. Think of yourself and your partner in terms of Mind-Body-Spirit connections. Control your orgasms, men especially; postpone ejaculation until you want that type of closure. Create a deep and spiritual connection with not only your partner but also with the Universe at large; use your meditation skills as you make love."

As I looked around the living room I saw a glazed look in some eyes. I said, "Do we have to get it perfect?"

Alyssa tossed her head back and laughed aloud. "Oh, dear me, no!" she exclaimed. "I've been practicing and I use that word purposefully practicing for thirty years and perfection is a nice unattainable goal. The journey is so enjoyable though. All of you should enjoy the journey."

"My bringing Alyssa here was to make you all aware of some new dimensions in yourselves and in your lovemaking that could heighten your feelings for each other. This shouldn't be an onerous chore; this should be fun," Noah interjected.

"When we reconvene tomorrow morning say ten o'clock, let's talk about how we each laughed and what struck us funny about this whole process. Remember sex is has three purposes: procreation not a focus for us now except Melissa." We all laughed. She finished her sentence then, "Pleasure a major focus for you all tonight; and Spiritual connection to your partner and the Universe also a focus for you all tonight. Don't worry the act to death. Just try to put it all together." She laughed again.

The rest of us in the room visibly relaxed.

"As I did last night, I will join some or all of you over the night," Alyssa added, "Not for instruction but for participation and my own pleasure and spiritual connection to you all. I love you all so much, I want to crawl inside every one of you and be close." She made a gesture of hugging herself on our behalf.

I stood and walked across the living room and took Alyssa in my arms and hugged her tightly. Alex stood and joined me, then Noah, then Doug, and soon everyone in the room stood surrounding Alyssa in one large group hug fifteen of us.

We formed pairs for the night again: Greg and Tiffany coupled by making ga-ga eyes at each other at the thought of being together for the night; Doug and Amy found one another and he went and sat next to her; Jeremy and Beth paired by simply sitting next to one another and holding hands; Noah and Jennifer paired with a short kiss and hug; Brad and Melissa with an embrace and an affectionate kiss by Brad on her bulging stomach; and Mark and Alex joined up with a kiss and hug.

As the pairings were made, David came to me and pulled me to a standing position. He said, "Avery, will you be mine tonight. I've wanted to be with you again for months and I can't believe I have this rare opportunity." David smiled and I melted into his arms and we kissed, the steam rising from our embrace.

Again, we drove all the cars into the small city and found a restaurant that would take our party of fifteen. Alyssa had us do 'food play' again as a form of foreplay. David and I had melted brie as an appetizer and did well pleasing each other with the slices of apple piled with brie. At one point we laughed so hard we attracted the attention of the whole restaurant.

I sat in David's lap in the car on the way back to the villa. Mark and Alex shared the back seat with us. Soon Alex and my short skirts were pulled up to our waists as our men stroked our naked pussies. Neither Alex nor I had worn underwear in anticipation of such an event.

Our temperatures rose, our sexual temperatures, as David's fingers stroked and penetrated around my nether region. We kissed and hugged all the way home. At one point, however, I noticed a different feel to the caresses of my clit. I turned to find that Mark and Alex were taking turns fingering me as David fingered Alex's sweet cunt.

I joined in our back seat swap by adding a finger deep into Alex's tunnel, her eyes rolling up in her head as David and I simultaneously sank our digits into her body. She and Mark returned the favor as our sexual temperatures rose.

Jennifer watched from the front seat as she stroked Noah's cock through his shorts. Noah adjusted the rear-view mirror so he could keep tabs on our sexual shenanigans. I teased him a bit by often flashing my pussy to him, as we'd pass beneath a bright streetlight, sometimes with someone's fingers embedded inside me.

Chapter Thirty-Two

At the house, I gave Noah a deep kiss and reminded him that I loved him and encouraged him to have a wonderful sexual encounter with his sister. I told him to really try to follow Alyssa's teaching and create 'Spiritual Sex.' He told me the same and we turned to our partners.

I started for the stairway to the bedroom, however David turned to me and softly said, "Not that way." He held my hand and led me from the large foyer to the Villa outside to the pool deck. Doug and Amy were stripping off their clothing for a swim as we walked by. Sexual being that I am I couldn't help but admire Doug's tumescent cock and Amy's little body.

David led me to the stone stairs and down them to the beach. Along the way we picked up a couple of large beach towels and carried them with us. We walked about a hundred yards up the beach in the near darkness that made up the night sky.

David stopped and we spread out the towels. Next, he came to me and gently pulled the few items of clothing I wore from my body, carefully piling them on one of our blankets. I repeated the process for him, leaving the two of us nude.

We walked together into the lazy surf that massaged the shoreline without any intent to inflict impact other than the rustling sound of the small wavelets. We floated and swam for a few minutes in the warm waters.

As we left the Caribbean and headed back to our towels, we both noted a rising crescent moon. In the darkness of the western sky, the moon seemed positively brilliant to me, and I turned and could see my moon shadow on the sand.

"Sit beside me and let's meditate for a while," David said. I sat and David came next to me. We both sat Indian style, our legs crossed but not in the severity of the lotus position. We interlaced our arms so we could touch one another and then focused on the stars on the far horizon.

My mind initially drifted, and I thought of what I hoped to do with David to bring him pleasure and joy in our union. Another thought went through my head about whether Alyssa would be able to find us. Next, I thought about the star near the horizon, and I focused on it and watched the games my eyes could play with the speck of light.

Finally, I had a few minutes of serenity where I really think I thought of nothing. A feeling of supreme well being swept through me several times, almost like mental orgasms rather than physical ones.

David pulled me from my reverie with a kiss. I kissed my readiness back to him. He uncurled his legs pulled me into his lap, his rising cock finding the lips of my pussy. I reached between us and pushed his cock against the moistness of my pussy, coating his rod with my juices.

"Lie back and look at the stars, Avery. Count them and think that every star is a place in the Universe that loves you." He helped me lie back.

David loved my breasts for a long time as I stroked his hair and upper body. Then as I focused on the Andromeda galaxy, David slid lower on my body until his tongue caressed my lower lips and my juices started to flow faster. Occasionally he'd flick his tongue across my clit. He had my attention.

"David," I told him softly in a loving voice, "I'm looking up at Andromeda. Somewhere in that galaxy of a billion stars, there's a sun with planets around it like ours, and on one of those planets two beings are lying beside a warm beach in a gentle breeze just the way we are, and they're making love. The female being is lying on her back as her male partner brings her orgasms and pleasures far beyond any pleasure we can imagine on earth. But she's looking up at the sky as her partner ministers to her, seeing a far-off galaxy called the Milky Way and she's imagining a sun with a planet like earth, and a sea like the Caribbean with two lovers beside it making love. And in this thought, we four lovers are connected with each other and in love."

He made me cum a couple of minutes later. I never shut my eyes; I just looked up at Andromeda and sent outward my feelings and wishes for passion, love and connectedness. I felt them echo around the Universe in my orgasm and return to me a hundred-fold.

David held me and we looked at the stars for a while. I brought David to a dry orgasm, praising him for his selfcontrol. "I'm looking at Andromeda, seeing the same couple and feeling their love," he told me.

"Avery, there are millions of loving people out there doing what we're doing. We're all connected," came and joined him. He waved his arm across the sky, "Right now, instantly across all the light years we see. We are here and in a million other places."

I heard someone walking down the beach toward us. Alyssa's voice found us first, "David, my love, you are right, and your observation is profound. You are connected to the spaces, things and beings you imagine in a million other places and they to you and to you Avery. Your pleasure is their pleasure, and their pleasure is your pleasure if you open yourself to receive it."

Alyssa's nude body slid between us on the blanket of towels we'd created. The bright moon lit her dark skin with a mystical light, creating a wondrous view of her figure through the shadows and shading the light made. She lay back and extended her arms to the sky above. "Caress the sky; reach for infinity," she told us, and we duplicated her move.

"Let me hold you both, love you both, provide a channel between the two of you and all the infinite possibilities the Universe is providing you," Alyssa said softly.

We let her wrap her arms around us. Somehow the connection became more than just her holding us, it became the essence of total and unbelievable sexual and erotic contact. I felt swept into her mind and felt my body give itself over to her.

I soared into my place of infinite and continuous orgasms so rapidly my head swam in the delicious joy of the occasion. I could feel penetration by David ... and Alyssa ... and Noah ... and, Oh My God, the entire world. It was wondrous!

I floated through space watching the stars go by, staring back at earth and realizing my place, our place in the reality of love that made up the Universe.

My erotic experience went on for hours and hours.I couldn't count the orgasms or the places in time and space that I occupied during those hours were one long continuous orgasm a single lasting spasm of pleasure, not just of my own but all the others that were connected to this place.

Chapter Thirty-Three

Hours passed and then I relinquished my grip on the zone of hedonistic pleasure I'd lived in. An aura of afterglow gradually descended upon me.

I blinked my eyes open, still at the edge of pleasure. The dawn lit the eastern sky and provided sufficient light to see around us. David's engorged cock penetrated my pussy, yet he seemed frozen in time as I'd been. I pushed against him to let him know I was awake, and he started to move into the reality I had found. His eyes blinked as he looked and me and then kissed me deeply. "Avery, I love you so. I've just had the most memorable night of my life," David said.

"David, I love you too. I too had an unreal experience all night. Alyssa came to us hours and hours ago. I think we spent the night with her. I ... I had ... We had one long continuous orgasm."

"I did too. I didn't know I could cum like that or climax with the feeling never ending," David said.

We hugged for a long time and tried to explain the experiences we had both had. As the dawn continued to brighten, we rose and slipped into the Caribbean, letting the warm waters wash over our nude bodies again. I thought of the analogy of being a wave in the ocean of infinite love. We gathered our belongings and walked down the beach to the stone stairway up to the Villa and ascended to the pool deck. Doug and Amy sat beside each other, their feet dangling in the pool. They were nude and having a very serious conversation.

"May we join you," I asked tentatively.

"Oh, yes. Please," Amy exclaimed as she awoke to our arrival. Doug nodded.

As we sat, Amy said to us, "Doug and I had the most amazing experience last night. We spent the night with Alyssa, and we just seemed to cum and cum and cum. I rose into an orgasm shortly after she joined us, and it didn't end until just a little while ago. Doug had the same experience."

I looked at her for a long time to see if she joked and realized she was serious. "Amy, David and I had an identical experience." We just nodded at the wonder and mystery surrounding Alyssa again.

Noah and Jennifer appeared as the four of us sat in silence. Noah sat beside me and kissed me. He said, "Jennifer and I had a night ... an unusual night. The sex ... our orgasms ... never ended all night. The experience was spiritual and erotic and ... I just can't describe it."

"Alyssa?" I turned and asked.

"Yes," he said, "she was with us all night, almost guiding us on our Spiritual journey – our orgasmic journey."

Noah realized we were all nodding in agreement. "All of you?" he asked. We kept nodding.

Not much later Brad and Melissa, Mark and Alex, Greg and Tiffany as well as Jeremy and Beth verified, they'd had nearly identical experiences.

"Where is Alyssa?" I asked, realizing she'd given us all the most incredible experiences of our lives and she wasn't here for us to thank.

Noah went to look for her. He came back to the pool deck a few minutes later caring a short note.

"She left," he told us all. "She left a note for us. 'Thank you all for being such wonderful pupils. You all learned so quickly, I think in part because you all are so ready to share your love with one another and with the Universe. Now all you need to do is practice. There is nothing that happened over the past couple of days that you can't do for yourself. Thank you for sharing your experiences with me and allowing me into your pairings. Our paths will cross again, I promise you. Go with love. Namasté, Alyssa.'"

"Wow," I exclaimed. The others made equally amazed sounds about her departure and the note.

"How do you feel?" Noah asked me.

"I feel amazingly rested and at peace with the world. I know I had a truly spiritual experience and I'm still living in the afterglow of that experience. The sex David and I had was only part of what I'm still feeling something much, much deeper and more transformative happened. How about you?" I asked.

"I feel the same way," Noah said. "I would like to go someplace, just with you, and savor what happened last night. Take a walk with me down the beach?"

I put my bikini bottoms on again and Noah slipped into a thong bikini. I loved his suit because you could see the muscles and dimples of his tight ass as he walked. We stood at the bottom of the stone stairway and kissed for a long time before we started walking. I could feel the juices flow from my body in the sensual kiss.

I think we walked for five miles or more. We passed a few other people who were similarly clad as we were. We talked little and thought a lot for a while. We held hands; we walked arm in arm; we walked with Noah's arm around my shoulder sometimes brushing against my breast and arousing my nipple. We swam a little in the aqua waters at a picturesque little cove we'd passed through.

"What are you thinking?" I finally asked Noah during our walk.

"Several things all at once," Noah responded. "I'm thinking how much I love you and how you think. When we did that exercise, I felt I could see deep inside you in a way we'd never did before. I resonated with your comments, your comments about feeling close."

Noah went on, "I'm also hopeful the others will get the same value from this that I did years ago and that I plan on refreshing this week. I forgot more and more about this as I got wrapped up in grad school."

"Why do you say that?" I asked.

"The short exercises about intimacy and closeness only scratch the surface for where Alyssa can take us," Noah said. "The type of thinking we should do in order to have one of the most loving, intimate and complete marriages in the world. We'll continue learning with each other after the exercises she gives us this week. She's been studying most of her life and is still learning."

"What you talk about intimacy, love, closeness and all, wouldn't we find those anyway in our marriage?" I asked.

"Maybe and maybe not," Noah said. "I want our marriage to be really rich and wonderful for each of us. Expanding how we love each other is a large part of this and this is what Alyssa will teach us not only this week but in future sessions with her. Part of what I want is to move beyond 'western' thinking and embrace some of the great concepts they've learned in India and the Orient about lovemaking."

We walked a hundred yards as I thought.

"We have adopted a polyamorous lifestyle. There are other people that we love and that love us and not just one or two. We could drift around in that as a couple and take what happens, but I want our marriage to be more than the two of us drifting with our lovers. I want us to have the deepest, richest and most intimate of our relationships," Noah began again without a question being posed "In all the dimensions we can think of, Mind-Body-Spirit is one set of dimensions, another might be the characteristics of one's life, family, social, professional or career, sexual fulfillment, intellectual fulfillment, recreational and play, relationships, financial and prosperity, motivations and health. You might think of others too."

"You mean we're close in all these areas?" I asked.

"As a goal, yes," he said. "To find completeness in some area you will want involvement of others in some way, hopefully from within our circle. But our aspiration is to be the best for each other in these areas. Otherwise, someone that knows all our relationships and us will ask someday, "Why'd you bother to get married?"

"Involving the others in Alyssa's education?" I asked.

"If we're going to have this polyamorous circle, I want the best for my lovers too. I think Alyssa and her philosophy can start each of us on a path a Spiritual journey that can enrich all of us." Noah began. "We'll all grow and evolve at different rates. We'll each internalize what we learn differently. Nonetheless, we'll all grow and share a common basis for loving and interacting with each other, and I like that. This is the direction I hope we'll all grow."

We walked some more and soon four ourselves back at the villa. We washed the salt water from our bodies in the dipping pool beside the beach and went up to join the others. The other women were sitting in loungers in the shade of a palm grove having an excited discussion about something. I could see Brad and David talking in the living room, occasionally laughing. Jeremy was bent over his laptop computer. The other men weren't around. Noah wandered towards the kitchen as I joined the circle of women.

"So you mean even if it's just masturbation we can bring ourselves to the same level of pleasure that we all found last night?" Amy talked with great animation in her voice.

"Yes, I think so. I mean if we each were to meditate and achieve some state of quiet, don't you think we could do that. We might have to kick start things with some stimulation, but I think I could you know, have a better experience," Tiffany responded.

"You mean you wouldn't be thinking of being the main subject of some all-night gang bang of hunky looking men?" Jennifer asked.

"No," Tiffany insisted with a wounded voice. "I know I've had my slutty times, but this isn't what I'm talking about. I really think if we were to get in a deep meditation we could 'ascend' the way Alyssa taught us. I wish she'd stayed; I have so much more to learn."

"When I meditated, I had a hard time making my mind go blank," Beth said. "I kept thinking of the kids, things I need to do, and on and on."

"You can get through that if you acknowledge the thought. One book I read said to say something to yourself like 'Thank you for sharing' and then pushing the unwanted thought away."

"I felt the same way," Alex volunteered. "When I started my mediation, my mind was all business. I made myself an observer of what my mind was thinking. Eventually I told my 'head' I'm going to take the 'real me' into a deeper and more spiritual place. Somehow I left the mundane things behind for a few minutes."

"I guess I'll have to keep trying," Beth said.

"Why don't we try it now?" Tiffany asked.

"What do you mean?" Amy asked.

"Let's all go off somewhere alone and masturbate. I mean have a 'Spiritual masturbation' just like we've been talking about. Meditate and focus on your own pleasure and on launching that pleasure into the Universe. If you need to use your fingers or vibrator, do so!"

"I'm close to having an orgasm just thinking about it." Melissa shook in delight, we laughed.

"I, for one, intend to try it," Tiffany announced as she stood.

"I'm in," I volunteered.

"Me too," Amy and Jennifer said.

"I'll try," Beth announced slowly.

"Me too and let's meet back here in ninety minutes and compare notes," Alex added.

I found Noah and told him I intended to slip away for a couple of hours. He nodded and told me he'd be reading somewhere around the house.

I went back down to the beach. As far as the eye could see the beach was empty. I removed my bikini bottom and set it on a patio table. I found a small footstool and set it beside the dipping pool looking out at the Caribbean. I adopted my meditative position, sitting Indian style. The added advantage in this case was that my sexual organs were fully available to me for caressing and stimulation.

Before I did more than just run my hands over my body in a sexy way, I found a small focus point near infinity the mountaintop of some distant cay, perhaps the Virgin Islands. I let this point absorb my thoughts and forced my needs, wants, worries and desires from my thinking. Gradually my head cleared. I became aware of the warm sun kissing my naked body and the sounds of the shore birds. I floated looking down at my body and a feeling of oneness with all the others, particularly my sisters in the Villa.

Somewhere, somehow, I felt the fingers of one hand penetrate my vagina and then pull the nectar our and spread it around my lips and clitoris. My other hand caressed and pinched my nipples. I soared into orbit. In hindsight I couldn't tell you if my eyes were open or closed. I lost all track of time.

There was only 'The Pleasure.'

I became connected with the Universe, with all of mankind, with the source of love and with Spirit itself. I entered the time and place of an endless orgasm. I know part of what I felt had to do with the manipulation and thrusting of my fingers and my palm across my clitoris or my search for my G-spot. Yet, I'd found some place and it had connection and pleasure not only with the physical but also with the Spiritual.

Over an hour later I sat alone in the shade of my palms reflecting on the pleasure I'd brought myself. Now I knew for sure that I could practice some of what Alyssa had left with us.

Like Tiffany, I felt I still had so much to learn.

The other women gradually drifted into the circle. We were all quiet but nodded to each other in us after glows. Even skeptical Beth smiled at her accomplishment.

"I have a question," I stated to the group. "If I wanted to create this state for one of you and you for me, could we do it together at the same time the way Alyssa did for us last night?"

"You mean a lesbian encounter?" Melissa asked.

I nodded in agreement.

"Let's eat some lunch and then try it. I'm curious and up for anything – but you men already know that!" Tiffany said. We all laughed at her statement.

We ate light lunches and over lunch paired off. I wanted to be with each of the women, so I had a hard decision. In the end, Alex, Amy and I formed a triad. The other pairs were Tiffany and Beth, and Jennifer and Melissa.

Alex, Amy and I went to our bedroom, throwing up the doors to the veranda and the magnificent view of the sea.

"Come and let's kiss one another," I insisted. Our trio merged tenderly and for many minutes we traded kisses, often using our tongues. As we kissed our fingers and hands roamed over each other's bodies, bringing nipples to erectness and fingering clits and plunging into vaginas. We all remained standing.

Eventually I pulled us all to the bed in a triangle. We sat as close as we could to one another, our knees touching yet our pussies fully exposed to the wondrous breezes circulating in the room. We held hands briefly but then abandoned that contact.

I put my head back and refocused on the small mountaintop, now invisible to sight but visible in my mind. I brought the thought of infinite and unconditional love into my mind, visualizing what that would be like and how I knew I'd soon feel immersed in that ocean. I thought of the pleasure I could bring the others which we'd bring each other; I thought how it would reverberate through the Villa and bring pleasure to the other women and men I loved.

I could feel a sense of Spiritual oneness sweep me up again. Love filled all space and time. As fingers caressed me, I brought pleasure to the others. My pleasure lifted me up and away from the physical world. I truly transcended and re-entered my state of orgasmic bliss. I knew this was heaven and all I'd needed to do all my life was open to the possibility that it was here now!

I lost track of time but when I found myself floating back to this reality, I sensed that two hours had passed. The sun had moved to a new location in the sky compared to when we started.

I looked with love at Alex and Amy. We kissed and hugged again. They too had shared in our mystical state of bliss.

"My God," Amy exclaimed, "If we were to package this and sell it, we could end wars and move planets."

"I can't believe I've spent most of the time since midnight in this orgasmic state. I hope Jeremy understands what's been happening and how it's affecting me," Alex offered.

"I feel I could pause almost anywhere and think myself into that state." I said, the others nodded in agreement. Try it," Alex softly urged.

I closed my eyes, thought of the warm water and the distant mountain, and drifted right up the scale to a place of ecstasy. Fingers darted across my clit, but they were unnecessary for my joy. I held the thoughts of heaven and love for several minutes and then relaxed back to consciousness.

"Wow," Amy said, "You really can just go right into it."

"You may become my new guru if Alyssa doesn't show up again." Alex said.

"As you achieved your climax state, you pulled us right up to the edge with you. Alex and I both touched each other and brought each other off, then we touched you, but you didn't seem to need us. I still feel so close to you both to everyone, Amy added. "Other times I'd want to crawl inside you but now I feel as though I am inside you both. I can't be closer." She touched us both in a sexual way.

We talked a little longer until there was a soft knock at the door from the porch. Noah stood there looking at the three of us.

"You three have had an amazing afternoon together. I hope you don't' mind but I sat and listened for a while," Noah said. "You were erotic, yet I knew you were all in a Spiritual place.

Mind, Body and Spirit really merged in this room."

I patted the bed beside me; Noah came and sat. "Do you want to make love with the three of us?" I asked him softly; he nodded. As I moved to kiss him, so did Amy and Alex.

Chapter Thirty-Four

After dinner at Le Galion, we returned to the beautiful Villa. That night Noah and I created our own Spiritual sex for one another. I drew great satisfaction in knowing that I could help him crest into an elevated state of continuous orgasm. I explained to Noah in more detail about what I'd learned from Alyssa and what I'd learned I could do during the afternoon before our quartet ended the afternoon in our bed. He filled me in on his learning too, showing me some techniques, he'd remembered.

Everyone in the Villa seemed to rise late the next day by design. Various combinations of people sunned, swam in one of the pools or the Caribbean Sea, read, toyed with their computer, read novels, and so forth. Two couples went shopping in town for a while. It was a lazy day and we all enjoyed it.

We ate at Beach Bar for dinner. We were about as dressed down as I thought we could be. I wore my bikini bottom and a thin white blouse tied in a knot beneath my tanned breasts.

Flip-flops completed my dinner ensemble. As it turned out, I was overdressed.

As we all funneled back into the villa after dinner, Jeremy announced that he had an erotic surprise for the bride and groom, and he was sure we'd be willing to share it with everyone.

"Come and gather around the big screen television," he instructed us all. We filed into the room and spread ourselves around on the various sofas and chairs as well as the floor. Lights were dimmed to enhance viewing of the huge flat screen television.

Jeremy stood before us all and the television screen came to life with a slow progression of photographs from the erotic photograph album, I gave Ben for Christmas months earlier, what I called 'Volume One'. I took it back from him after I found out about the lying and sleeping with a hard limit.

"Most of you have seen Avery's erotic photograph album. I'm pleased it sits on her coffee table as a continual reminder of her love for Noah and, of course, for my beautiful and sexy wife Alex." He paused and collected a small kiss from Alex.

"Before we start, there's no Ben in any of these photos is there?" I asked.

"No," he went on, "I am pleased to present for the first time Volume 2."

A slow classical music piece became audible in the background and then increased in volume until it filled the room with imposing music. More impressive, however, were the slow progression of photographs of first me, then me and Noah, making love to one another. Every shot was erotic in some way, a curve or flap of skin, a close up of my pussy damp in anticipation of lovemaking, a photo of an erect penis about to penetrate, a tongue arched to barely touch my clitoris.

The 'album' unfolded almost in a storyline of seduction, foreplay and then penetration in a wide variety of positions. After fifty or sixty photographs the scene shifted again to one of obvious after glow, my creamy pussy proof-positive of our climaxes.

The music ebbed and Jeremy stepped forward again in the dim light, "Of course, we took more photographs for other more albums as well. So here are Volumes Three and Four, if you will." He stepped aside and the classical music rose to match the scenes again.

This time the scene shifted, and Alex and I made love again. Visible in the photographs were our tongues and genitals pleasing one another, fingers penetrating, and the shadows and curves of our sexy bodies as we made love. As the photos projected on the screen I went and cuddled in the overstuffed chair with Alex, pulling our tops from our bodies so I could stroke her chest; then we shed everything so we could touch each other unimpeded. Other clothing in the room seemed to come off too.

A scene shift brought Noah into a threesome with Alex and me. Highly erotic shots of his cock buried in Alex's cunt, moist with her nectar as I licked, made half the room groan in sexual frustration that they weren't immediately copulating with someone. I watched as a nude Amy moved to my husband and sank her pussy down on Noah's steel rod. He grasped her breasts from behind as she started to slowly ride his cock.

Another scene shift occurred on the television screen and the threesome became a foursome, including Jeremy's remarkable photographs of his long cock deep in my pussy and then barely penetrating in the next, his mushroomed head all but breaking contact with my skin. I reached past Alex's shoulder and stroked his hardening cock through his thin shorts.

Somehow, he'd captured shots of all of us fucking, lined up along our living room sofa in Seattle, and then obviously changing partners multiple times for variety in our lovemaking. The last few photographs showed a progression of cum flowing from cocks into pussies, across breasts, into mouths, and even being shared between Alex and me. The scene shifted to some flowers on our coffee table and then faded as the classical music ended.

The silence in the room gave way to a standing ovation for Jeremy and Alex and their photographic work. They bowed their now nude bodies.

"Wait!" he said, "There's more! While we were doing the still photographs, we also had a video camera running most of the time. Now I haven't been able to edit this as much as I'd like but I wanted to share it with you all as it is."

He looked at the assemblage of half-naked horny people in the room and added, "Fucking while you watch this video is permitted and will be taken by the film crew as a positive gesture that you like the film." We laughed and I pulled down Jeremy's shorts and maneuvered him into my lap as the film began.

As I fondled Jeremy's rising cock, I watched the others forming pairs. Soon everyone had a partner. The video started with me seductively disrobing for Jeremy. I remembered that morning a week or so earlier when I'd found him before anyone else had awoken and we'd fucked. Now here was that complete erotic scene captured for posterity as I mouthed his cock, deep throating his rod, and then mounting him on our sofa. The fuck was memorable in particular because of my stream of 'dirty' talk to him, mostly telling him how excited I felt to be able to fuck Alex's husband and how I hoped that Noah's cock was right at that moment buried deep in Alex's pussy. These weren't forbidden acts, just something we were doing to satisfy each other's lust and to bring joy to the moment.

The scene shifted when Alex and Jeremy joined the party and then escalated again to more orgasms. Somewhere along the line Alex and I took turns lapping the cum our partners had left in our vaginas; usually we shared our discoveries.

Around the viewing room the slap of bodies together started to add to the erotic situations on the video. Even Noah and I started to grind into one another as the film progressed. Further, I found it such a turn on to be able to look around the room at seven couples in various stages of making love. I think, at heart, every one of us is an exhibitionist; the shows being put on for the benefit of the others boggled the mind.

The scene on the television eventually shifted to Noah and my bedroom. A long scene rolled by where I rode Jeremy's muscular body, my eyes closed, and my body focused on extracting my pleasure from him. I came multiple times, a precursor to what Alyssa taught us this week.

Next the television screen lit up with a close up of Noah's cock stroking in and out of Alex's ripe pussy. As he pumped into her, Alex's fluids flowed from her body. I could actually smell her body sex, then I realized that Alex and Doug were fucking right next to me. I reached over and inserted my hand between them, stroking and tickling Alex's clit to heighten her sensations.

On screen, Noah orgasmed into Alex's steaming pussy. Alex ejaculated too, a small jet of girl juice coating the two bodies.

Noah pulled away after filling her pussy and the camera zoomed in on Alex's pussy showing a rivulet of cum slowly oozing from her vagina and then running across her thigh towards the bed covers. The scene faded to black ending the tape.

The scene in the room did not change, however. Bodies still pumped into other bodies, and moans and groans were heard from one end to the other.

Then the orgasms started to arrive. Melissa surprised me by being the first to cum. On the cushy carpeting, David nestled behind her with his long cock solidly buried in her tunnel. Every stroke and twitch we could watch ... and did. Melissa's breasts were swollen from the pregnancy and David took delight in fondling and holding them as he pumped in her body and then as the two of them wallowed in the afterglow of their climaxes.

Noah and Amy climaxed, Amy falling back onto Noah's body as embraced her and kissed her neck and shoulders from her back. Amy looked so 'right' with Noah; I had a fleeting thought of her moving back to the U.S. from Paris and moving in with us. I'd like that and I know Noah would.

A wave of orgasms trickled across the room with bodies in many different positions and sounds coming from couple after couple. I thought how beautiful the act of lovemaking is regardless of time, circumstance, position, or inclination. Making love is an act of unity and spiritual achievement.

Alyssa was right; I hoped I'd see her again soon.

Chapter Thirty-Five

Noah and I again snuck away from the others after Jeremy's slide show and movie. We went down to the beach and walked, in the nude, for a while. When the urge struck, I lay back in the soft sand and Noah penetrated into me. Over his shoulder and with his knowledge, I merged with some unknown constellation and then soared across the Universe. Noah, too, entered a blissful state. I returned to earth awash in Noah's cum; further, I had apparently jetted my girl juice across his body in my orgasmic state.

After we cooed and cuddled, we swam in the warm sea then walked back to the Villa and went to bed, our nude bodies loosely wrapped around each other beneath the slowly churning ceiling fan.

I awoke the next morning to someone eating my pussy. I could tell it was a female and by process of elimination I figured out that it was Amy. I finally blinked my eyes opened and verified my guess.

"To what do I owe the honor of this occasion?" I asked in a sleepy, just waking up, voice.

"Just, I love you and I want to be close to you again," she said. Her tongue dove onto my clitoris and she thrust three fingers into my slot. I moaned loudly.

"But I'm not quite ready to return the favor," I stammered out and tried to reach for her attractive face. "I'm just waking up and in a wonderful way I might add."

"No reciprocity required. Just lie back and enjoy this. Sometime you can return the favor or Noah can." Noah lay next to me on his stomach apparently oblivious to the pleasure Amy delivered to me.

I allowed myself to drift with her attentions and then I knew an orgasm grew near. "Amy, I'm going to cum very soon. Don't stop. Oh, ... please ... don't ... stop!" I barely got the words out when deep inside my body I felt a sudden warmth and spasm that radiated outward, ending right at my clitoris and Amy's tongue.

"I love you. I love you. I love you," I moaned.

Amy came up and let me hold her in my arms. "Oh thank you," I told her as we kissed. "Do I have morning breath?" "You're fine," she said, kissing back. After a silent moment as I savored the event, she'd just delivered, Amy said, "I love you. I don't want our sexual times together to end. I've so enjoyed the past week. Wow has it only been a week? I hope you feel the same way."

"Don't worry Darling," I told her. "I'm here for you always in every way you can imagine."

"There's something else," Amy said. "I've really fallen for Greg. I think he feels the same way. I mean when we haven't been off with someone else, we've been together. He's such a special person and has so many great traits. Am I crazy? Is he as good as he appears to be?"

"Oh, Amy," I said, hugging her to me. "I hoped the two of you would 'click.' I love Greg and yes, he is all he appears to be and more. If I make a list of all the traits you'd want in a guy, Greg's got them, just like Noah. Plus, I think he can handle the emotions that being at a week like this can evoke without being overwrought."

"I'm so taken with him that I might ask for reassignment back to the U.S. from Paris. What do you think about that?"

"I think the whole world would rejoice to have you closer to us all," I told her.

"Then I'm going back and wake him up and tell him," Amy said almost asking for permission from me.

"Go for it," I told her. She stood, her nude form that of a goddess, and left the room.

Noah said in a clear voice from his sleep position, "I'd be very happy if she came back to the States. She can come visit us anytime."

"I'm glad you like my sister," I told him as I slipped into his open arms.

"No, I love your sister," he said with a grin. "And I'd like to love her many more times too."

The two of us made love again that morning.

I wore a bikini bottom to breakfast, in part to stem the flow of semen from my lower orifices. Several of the others were up and we availed ourselves of the wonderful assortment of fresh foods that had been left for our daytime meals. Soon Tiffany and I whipped up omelets for everyone with bacon and sausages on the side.

We all wiled away the day as we had the one before. Four men went golfing; a couple of the other women went shopping.

Melissa came and got me in mid-afternoon; I'd been reading beside the pool. She said, "Key family meeting on the beach in ten minutes." Now that piqued my curiosity, so I sashayed down the stone stairway at the appointed time, joining Jennifer and Tiffany around the lower swimming pool.

"What gives?" I asked as I sat beside the others on one of the large loungers.

Melissa said, "I need your advice and counsel before Mark and David get back from golf with the others."

We nodded. Tiffany asked, "Advice about what?"

"I've really fallen for David, I mean big time, my heart beats faster, palms go cold kind of fallen. I'm in love and I know he loves me; I mean really, really loves me. He loves my 'bump' too, my Avery." She shot me a grin knowing I was an obvious soft touch for my soon-to-be-born niece.

Melissa went on, "Now, I don't want to leave Mark or Tiffany, but I love David. Am I nuts? What should I do?"

Tiffany tossed her head back and laughed, "Oh, my Darling, Melissa. I love you so." She pulled Melissa next to her on the chaise they were on and kissed her.

Jennifer and I laughed too. Finally, Tiffany said the words we were all thinking, "Have David join the three of you. He likes, and even loves Tiffany too. He's a pal with Mark. He does work about 500 miles away but I'm sure you'll figure out a solution to that. Just ask him."

Jennifer and I nodded our concurrence with the suggestion.

Melissa looked shocked. "I never thought I could have my cake and eat it too – so to speak," she gave a lewd grin. "Do you think he'd buy it?

"You won't know until you ask?" I said, "But I do suggest you talk to Mark first." She agreed.

We swam in the Caribbean, Melissa sitting in the sand letting the gentle waves break over her engorged stomach. I stood and laughed with the others at her plight as a wave broke over her belly. She replied, "I'm teaching Avery to get used to the water."

Two hours later I saw Melissa waylay Mark as he came back from the golf game, pulling him off to their bedroom for a private time. Tiffany, Jennifer and I smiled at one another. The pair didn't reappear for almost two hours and Melissa had that 'just fucked' look about her as well as a smile on her face.

Mark looked pretty happy too.

The cocktail hour arrived only this time the four pilots amongst us opted out from drinking alcoholic beverages. This was our last night on St. Martens, and we'd all be departing in our aircraft the next morning.

As we sat around nursing some Diet Cokes, I watched Melissa lead David away from the group and back down the stairway to the beach. The sky was awash with reds and oranges as the sun set. Noah, Mark and Brad got the large grill going and soon we started preparing various elements of our cookout meal.

Steaks eventually went on the grill. The attractive odor of grilled beef filled the patio and wafted everywhere within two hundred yards. I thought Melissa and David should appear momentarily to see what we were cooking. I was wrong.

We saved them food but the rest of us started to eat at the huge, long table that seated all fourteen of us. Two seats were empty.

Eventually as we were finishing, David and Melissa appeared.

I knew she'd been successful in recruiting him to a new foursome; she had a smile from ear to ear as well as that freshly fucked look again. David looked pleased too.

Tiffany stood and went to David and kissed him deeply and with great meaning. She hugged him. I heard her welcome him to their family. Mark was there too with a bear hug and a strong handshake. The rest of us lined up to congratulate the four of them.

"I have so many questions. I don't even know some of the questions to ask. I do know this feels so right to be doing this and I love Melissa so ... and Tiffany ... and Mark ... and all of you." David and Melissa both had tears in their eyes as they hugged again.

Chapter Thirty-Six

The fourteen of us stood between the two jets hugging and kissing each other. Two linemen stood ready to assist us in leaving the ramp area at St. Maarten's airport, amazed at the intimacy we all shared with each other as we kissed and hugged goodbye. Eventually we broke apart, whispered our love for each other once more, and boarded one of the two jets.

Greg and David's Learjet filled with Melissa, Tiffany, Mark, Brad, Jennifer, Beth and Doug. I watched from the pilot-in-command seat as David waved to us one last time and folded up the electric stairs and secured the door. We waited while they started their engines and ran through their checklists and then left the pad to taxi to the runway for takeoff.

Noah sat in our co-pilot's seat. In the back of the plane were Amy, Jeremy and Alex. Jeremy and Alex would catch an evening red-eye back to London that night. Amy would spend a few more days in New Hampshire with our parents before spending a night with us and flying back to Paris.

Noah had gotten himself a new plane before we left, you know, for business purposes. The radio came alive in my headset, "Citation, November-Four-Eight-Gulf (our tail number),

Clearance Delivery." Noah replied and they started again, "November-Four-Eight-Gulf is cleared to Charlie-Echo-Delta airport in the United States, via RNAV Direct Juliet-AlphaX-Mark, Direct. Vectors after departure. Expect Flight Level 410 five minutes after. And you are cleared to taxi to Runway 09; hold short landing traffic." I let Noah repeat the clearance back to them as I set up the radios with the correct frequencies and put the waypoints in the Global Position System.

We taxied to the runway and went through our checklists. I found my confidence returning stronger than ever. Noah and I smiled at each other, and he reached over and gave me a loving squeeze of my right shoulder. We watched a Boeing 757 sweep into a landing, roll-out, and then taxi towards the commercial terminal.

The radio came alive again, "November-Four-Eight-Gulf cleared for take-off. After take-off, turn to flight plan route and cleared to Flight Level 410. Contact departure on one-twoeight-decimal-niner-five after clearing one thousand." Noah repeated the instructions back as I revved up the engines and started to taxi the last few feet to position the plane on the runway.

I took a quick look back at our passengers. Alex was already asleep. Jeremy and Amy were holding hands. Amy gave me a thumbs up gesture of support and confidence with a big smile.

The Citation turned to the runway heading and then we started our roll down the 7,070-foot runway. We soared flawlessly into the air well before the end and I repeated the climb-out checklist from memory.

As we cleared ten thousand feet on a nearly cloudless day, I gestured for Amy to come up and join us in the jump seat. She came and sat, asking us to explain in detail each of the flight instruments and radios. She seemed fascinated with everything we showed her.

"You know I wouldn't mind becoming a pilot," Amy told us as we eventually made our turn nearly eight miles high over Jacksonville. "Maybe Greg will teach me how to fly.

About the Author

Tammy Godfrey has called Southeast Idaho home for the vast majority of her life. She survived sixteen years in the military, and she is proud of almost every minute of it. After leaving the camouflage uniform behind she decided she needed to do something productive with the time that she wasn't taking care of her husband and kids. When she wasn't lost in the exciting world of tax preparation, she was hitting the books at Idaho State University seeking a degree in something practical like business. During her time in the world of academia she discovered a love for writing. After spending long days and nights overcoming her fear of the blank page her first book was published in 2013. She is currently working hard on her next novel. Tammy loves everything geek, including her adorable husband, and loves working on crafty things, reading, and going to comic con. Tammy believes that Murphy's Law has played a large part in her life. If anything, weird can happen, it will. One thing that can be said about Tammy Godfrey, she's not boring.

You can connect with me on:
https://www.facebook.com/tammy.godfrey.735

Also by Tammy Godfrey

Murder on the Morning Mist

Natalie Hart was a divorced mother of four. The four kids have grown and left the small town of Bear Lake, the ex-husband has not. Having her ex, and the woman he cheated on her with, living in the same town was just one of several issues that plaque Nat's thoughts every morning when she goes out on a run. There's the family Inn that she tries to manage, and a family curse that she tries to forget. Nat began her typical day with a typical run, expecting to find what she always found, a brisk mountain breeze, squirrels in the trees, and the stillness of the calm lake. It's the lake that brings the tourists, and they bring the money that keeps the town going. But the one thing Natalie Hart didn't expect to find could change the town forever. It will bring danger and mystery, bad boys from the recent past, and treasures from long past. It will reveal secrets, and those who want the secrets kept. You should be careful when you go for a run in the morning mist, you never know what you're going to find, and you may never stop running.

Milton Keynes UK
Ingram Content Group UK Ltd.
UKHW040234031224
451863UK00001B/29